Caught in Alaska

Caught in Alaska

Alaina Robbins

To my mom, thank you for always reading my drafts
(and for raising me, obviously).

1

The plan was to catch a glimpse of Alaska's wild beauty, not to be caught up in something even wilder. But as I stared into his deep blue eyes, I couldn't help but get transported back to the rugged wilderness and excitement of my past.

Five Years Ago

I pressed my forehead against the plane window, watching the city shrink beneath a patchwork quilt of concrete and asphalt. Excitement bubbled in my chest, mixed with the faintest flutter of nerves. This trip had been a dream in the making—Juneau, Alaska, with its sweeping landscapes and wild adventures, was about to become our reality.

Across the aisle, Cassie was engrossed in a travel guide, her brow furrowed in concentration. Sarah was fidgeting in her seat, her curly hair bouncing with every movement. I could almost feel her energy radiating from the other side of the row.

"Did you see this?" Cassie said suddenly, flipping the book around for us to see. "There's a hike that leads to a waterfall in the valley! We have to do it."

"Count me in!" Sarah exclaimed, her eyes lighting up. "I can already picture us swimming in the glacial water. It'll be freezing, but totally worth it."

I grinned, feeling the rush of their enthusiasm wash over me. "As long as we have towels to dry off with afterward," I said, trying to keep the practical part of my brain engaged.

I opened my laptop and began typing, recounting the events that had taken place so far on our trip. From a delayed flight to a spilled coffee, our journey had started out eventful, to say the least. I had begun working on my newest project. My newest addition to a line of travel books from my adventures. This one would be no different. Stories from my time here, anecdotes from my experiences, interactions with fellow travelers, and even locals. I wanted to capture what it was really like in each place that I visited.

"Look at that!" Sarah pointed, her finger tracing the outline of a distant glacier. "It's stunning!"

As we landed, the thrill of anticipation surged through me. The plane rolled to a stop, and the cabin buzzed with excitement. We gathered our bags, hearts pounding as we prepared to disembark.

Stepping off the plane, the crisp air greeted us, a refreshing change from the stale cabin atmosphere. The smell of pine and sea salt mixed in the air, invigorating and new. Juneau was alive with a buzz of energy, a small town nestled between mountains and ocean.

I let my long brown hair down from its ponytail and zipped up my black jacket, trying to get some reprieve from the cold day. The sun was out, which helped, but it was still too cold for my taste. Thankfully, it wasn't raining. I had heard horror stories about people who came here in the off-season. But as I looked around, all I could see were beautiful wildflowers in shades of pink and purple. Lupine and fire-weed, I had read in my travel guide.

"I can't believe we're really here!" I exclaimed, looking around at the quaint airport bustling with travelers.

"Let's find our rental yacht!" Cassie chirped, leading the way toward the baggage claim.

With our bags in tow, we made our way outside, where a shuttle bus awaited us, ready to take us to the harbor. The short ride gave us a glimpse of our surroundings, vibrant murals painted on the sides of buildings, the scent of fresh seafood wafting through the air, and locals waving hello as we passed by.

Once we arrived at the harbor, the sight of the Northern Light brought a rush of exhilaration. The yacht bobbed gently against the dock, its white exterior gleaming in the late afternoon sun.

"There she is!" Sarah exclaimed, pointing excitedly.

"Let's get settled in and then explore!" I suggested, the weight of the world lifting as the thrill of adventure settled into my bones.

We hurried aboard, the excitement of our Alaskan journey just beginning to unfurl. Little did I know, it wouldn't just be the breathtaking landscapes that would capture my heart on this trip.

The air was cooler than expected as I stepped onto the deck of the Northern Light, the rented yacht that would carry us through the Alaskan Inside Passage. The water was smooth beneath us, a glassy reflection of the mountains that rose, snow-dusted, from the shore. I'd been anticipating this trip for months, and finally, we were here, breathing in the scent of salt and pine.

"Can you believe we're actually doing this?" Sarah said, her eyes wide as she leaned over the railing.

Beside her, Cassie was already snapping pictures of the coastline, a dedicated traveler's checklist in hand. I'd made this trip with my best friends, wanting to escape from the routine back home and chase a bit of the wild. We'd saved up, researched every stop on the itinerary, and somehow found this yacht that fit our budget—small, charming, and full of rustic Alaskan character.

The excitement simmered beneath the surface of my thoughts as I turned to go inside, thinking I'd grab a drink and settle in. But as soon as I stepped into the main cabin, my gaze landed on someone who didn't exactly fit the yacht's quiet, wood-paneled aesthetic.

He was behind the bar, arranging a row of glasses, his hands moving with a practiced ease. Dark hair, a day's stubble, and eyes that, in the dim light, looked like they were hiding something. A well-worn fisherman's bracelet wrapped his wrist, and when he looked up and caught me staring, he raised an eyebrow, half amused, half curious.

"Welcome aboard," he said, voice warm and edged with something that sounded suspiciously like sarcasm. "You must be the tour group."

"That's us," I replied, gathering up the poise I could muster. "Thanks for having us on board."

His mouth tugged into a smirk as he leaned forward, wiping his hands on a rag. "Name's Jack. I'm the bartender, unofficial guide, and sometimes, if you're lucky, storyteller. Anything to drink?"

I hesitated, watching his hands as they found a bottle on the counter. "Surprise me."

Jack nodded, casting a quick, assessing look my way, then started pouring. "What brings you to Alaska?" he asked as he mixed my drink. "Not many people come this far up just for fun."

I laughed. "Guess we're not most people. We're here for adventure, wildlife, a break from normal life."

He slid the drink across the counter, his gaze lingering. "Adventure, huh? Well, I hope Alaska lives up to your expectations."

There was a trace of a challenge in his voice, like he was daring me to prove I could handle whatever Alaskan wildness we encountered. I picked up the drink, noting the slight blush of cranberry, a hint of citrus, the sprig of something green floating on top. It was refreshing and unexpected, much like the man who'd made it.

"To Alaska," I said, raising the glass.

"To Alaska," he echoed, a slow smile forming. "Let's hope she's gentle with you."

As the boat hummed to life, I realized this trip was already delivering more than I'd planned—an introduction to the rugged land, a drink with a stranger, and a thrill I couldn't quite name.

As soon as we finished stashing our bags in the cramped little cabin, I practically bounced into the hallway, pulling the others along with me. The air felt charged, like we were about to uncover some hidden treasure in every nook of the ship.

The walls were a deep, polished wood, and each narrow doorway led to cabins that seemed so cozy they might burst with charm. The hum of the boat's engine, mixed with the faint scent of salt and sea, reminded me that this was really happening. Alaska was waiting for us.

I took the lead, pausing at a little brass-rimmed window to peek out at the harbor before heading up a narrow staircase. It creaked with each step, giving the boat a rustic, storied feel, as if it had seen a hundred adventures before ours. When we finally reached the deck, I stopped dead in my tracks, struck by the view.

"Oh, wow," I whispered.

The harbor was stunning, a postcard come to life. Fishing boats rocked gently on the water, backed by a line of pine-green mountains that seemed to reach straight into the sky.

Colorful buildings dotted the shoreline of Juneau, snug against each other like they were huddling for warmth.

Cassie leaned over the railing, her long hair whipping around her face in the breeze. "This is insane. I feel like we're in some dream vacation ad."

"I didn't know the boat would be this nice," I murmured, my eyes sweeping over the upper deck. There were little seating areas set up with cushioned benches and deck chairs, all waiting to be claimed for lazy afternoons. I could already picture myself curled up there with a book, or staring out into the ocean, scanning the waves for signs of whales or seals.

Just then, a voice pulled us from our awestruck moment. I turned to see a young guy with sandy blond hair and a clipboard making his way toward us. He wore the ship's logo embroidered on his polo shirt and greeted us with an easy smile.

"Hi, welcome aboard! I'm Trevor, your steward for the trip," he said, gesturing for us to follow him. "If you're interested, I'd be happy to show you around."

He led us back inside to the lounge, a cozy space lined with soft sofas, nautical décor, and windows that offered views of the harbor. A spread of snacks and drinks had been set out on a little table. I grabbed a glass of water, trying to ground myself in the reality of the moment. Was I really here? It was like I'd stepped into the middle of an adventure novel.

Trevor pointed to a shelf lined with board games and books. "We've got some entertainment options here, and for those of you looking to explore, we keep a few kayaks stored at the back. We'll be making several stops, so you can get off, explore, and even paddle around some of the bays."

Cassie gave me a wide-eyed look, and I could see she was just as excited as I was. Kayaking in Alaska—that was something I hadn't even dared to dream about.

With a quick rundown of safety tips and meal plans, Trevor wrapped up the tour and left us to settle in. As he walked away, I took a deep breath, absorbing everything around me. This was going to be one incredible adventure—I could feel it. And I couldn't wait to see what Alaska had in store.

After a quick stop back in the cabin to grab our purses, the three of us headed out onto the docks, eager to start exploring. The harbor was bustling, full of life and color as boats rocked gently in their moorings, and the faint scent of fish mingled with the crisp sea air. The sky stretched wide and clear, a soft Alaskan blue, and it felt like the start of something big.

Cassie pointed toward a little row of shops lining the waterfront. "I say we start there and work our way down," she said, practically vibrating with excitement.

"I'm in," I replied, leading the way down the wooden pier. Each shop looked as inviting as the last, their windows filled with displays of cozy sweaters, carved totems, and local art. There was something about the place that felt like a perfect mix of rustic charm and wild adventure, and it was impossible not to feel the pull to see everything.

We wandered through a small gift shop first, where Cassie bought a little carved bear, "for good luck," she said, rubbing its head with a grin. We spent the next hour hopping in and out of stores, picking up little mementos—a tiny silver salmon necklace for Sarah, a plush puffin for me. I'd never been one for souvenirs, but something about these little things made me want to remember every second of this trip.

Once we'd seen every last shop on the dock, we piled into a rental car and drove into the heart of downtown Juneau. The city was a blend of colorful storefronts, historic buildings, and rugged natural backdrops, all framed by the towering mountains that made everything feel both small and safe.

The main street was filled with locals and tourists alike, bundled in jackets and beanies, some carrying freshly brewed coffee cups or clutching bags of pastries. As we passed a small bakery, Cassie practically skidded to a halt, her eyes lighting up.

"Oh, we have to go in here!" she said, already heading toward the door before we could answer.

Inside, the warm smell of baked bread and cinnamon wrapped around us. A chalkboard menu listed specialties like smoked salmon bagels and wild berry tarts. I grabbed a steaming coffee and one of the tarts, taking a moment to savor the flaky, buttery crust and sweet burst of berry with every bite. Cassie and Sarah chatted away, laughing as they shared bites of different pastries.

"This is... amazing," Sarah said, brushing crumbs from her sweater as she took in the scene around us.

After a while, we wandered further down the street and found ourselves in front of the Alaska State Museum. With its sleek architecture, it looked a bit out of place amidst the older buildings, but I'd read that it was packed with Alaskan history, from Indigenous artifacts to displays about the Gold Rush.

"Should we go in?" Cassie asked, glancing at us with that familiar glint in her eyes.

"Absolutely," I nodded, feeling a strange tug. I wanted to know this place, to feel like more than just a tourist.

Inside, the exhibits were incredible—colorful woven baskets, carvings that told stories of the Tlingit and Haida people, and clothing crafted to survive Alaska's harsh winters. I found myself lingering by a display about sea life, studying the models of orcas and seals as if they could tell me secrets about the water we'd be sailing over in just a few days. It felt like, with every step we took through these exhibits, we were becoming a little more connected to this wild, beautiful land.

When the light started to dip, casting a golden glow over everything, we headed back toward the harbor, feeling a little more tired but a lot more alive. I couldn't shake the feeling that this was just the beginning of something incredible—not just the sights we'd see, but the memories we'd make and the sense of wonder that seemed to grow with every new view.

As we climbed back aboard the boat, I looked over the harbor once more, a quiet thrill rising in my chest. This was exactly where I was meant to be.

We were stopped in the hallway by a dark-haired man with a thick mustache and beard. He had dark brown eyes and a stocky build, and seemed right at place here on the boat.

"Hello there, my name is Captain Lewis and I'll be taking us out on our adventure in the morning. Did you ladies get a chance to explore the town a bit?"

"We did! It's beautiful here," I replied.

"Glad to hear you're liking it so far. When we get back from our tour of some nearby stops, I'll have Jack, the bartender and guide, show you around to some of the local spots," he said with a grin.

"That sounds perfect! I can hardly wait," Cassie said.

Getting to explore more of Alaska, go to the local spots, and with Jack at that, sounded like just what I needed. I smiled politely and ducked into my cabin.

* * *

The sun had begun to dip below the horizon, casting a warm golden glow through the large windows of the small cabin where we were having dinner. I sat at the rustic wooden table with Sarah and Cassie, excited but still a bit anxious about our first evening in Alaska. The cabin smelled of fresh herbs and grilled fish, a delightful reminder of the beauty of the place we were in.

"Are you sure this guy is as cute as you say he is?" Cassie asked, smirking as she fiddled with the cocktail shaker that Jack had left on the counter.

"Absolutely," I replied, trying to sound more confident than I felt. "I mean, he's a local guide. He knows all about the area, and he has this... rugged charm."

"Rugged charm? Is that code for 'he probably has a beard'?" Sarah teased, raising an eyebrow.

"Maybe," I laughed, rolling my eyes playfully. "But you'll see for yourselves soon enough. Besides, he's making us drinks, so we should give him a chance."

Just then, the door swung open, and Jack walked in, carrying a tray filled with glasses and a bottle of something that sparkled in the fading light. He looked relaxed in a simple T-shirt and shorts, his hair slightly tousled from the wind. "Ladies, I hope you're ready to be impressed," he said, his voice warm and inviting.

"Are you going to show us how to make the famous Alaskan cocktails?" Cassie asked, her eyes glinting with mischief.

"Something like that," he replied, flashing us a grin that made my heart flutter. "I've got a special mix just for you."

As he poured the drinks, I couldn't help but watch him, the way he moved effortlessly around the kitchen, confident and at ease. The atmosphere felt charged, like we were part of a scene from a movie. He filled our glasses with a vibrant mix of colors and added a sprig of mint to each one, then set them down on the table with a flourish.

"Here you go," Jack said, leaning against the counter. "This one's a berry fizz. Made with fresh raspberries and a little bit of lime juice. It's my favorite summer drink."

"Wow, this looks amazing!" Sarah exclaimed, picking up her glass and taking a sip. "It tastes even better than it looks!"

I raised my glass, feeling a thrill of excitement. "To Alaska and new adventures," I said, and we clinked our glasses together. "And to our amazing bartender!"

"Cheers!" Jack echoed, his eyes locking onto mine for just a moment longer than necessary. I felt a rush of warmth in my cheeks.

As we settled into dinner, the conversation flowed easily. We shared stories about our lives back in New York, and Jack shared tales of his adventures guiding tourists through the wild landscapes of Alaska. Each story was more captivating than the last, and I found myself leaning in closer, hanging on his every word.

"Have you ever had a really close encounter with a bear?" Sarah asked, her eyes wide with curiosity.

Jack chuckled, running a hand through his hair. "Oh, absolutely. The first time was during one of my early trips. We stumbled upon a mama bear with her cubs. It was thrilling, but I made sure to keep my distance. Always respect the wild."

"You're really brave," I said, surprised at how much admiration I felt for him. "I don't know if I could handle that."

"Bravery is all about perspective," he said, his gaze steady. "What scares some people just makes others feel alive."

As he spoke, I caught a glimmer of something deeper in his eyes, a shared understanding that sparked a connection I hadn't anticipated. I felt my heart race, the flirtation hanging in the air like a promise.

"Okay, Mr. Brave Guide," Cassie said, interrupting my thoughts. "What do you have planned for us while we're here?"

Jack leaned closer, his tone playful. "How about a hike to a hidden waterfall? It's a bit of a trek, but the view is absolutely worth it."

"Count us in!" Sarah replied enthusiastically, her excitement palpable.

"Great. But I warn you, I'm not responsible for any of your gasps of awe," he joked, a teasing glint in his eye.

"I think we can handle a little awe," I said, matching his playful energy. "As long as you promise to keep the cocktails coming."

Jack laughed, the sound warm and infectious, and I knew in that moment that this trip was going to be unforgettable. With each shared glance and lighthearted banter, I felt the chemistry between us deepen, a spark of something new igniting. I couldn't shake the feeling that this was just the beginning of a remarkable adventure.

By the time I was ready for bed I felt comforted by the gentle sounds of the water slapping across the hull of the boat. Before long, I drifted to sleep dreaming about the gorgeous views and rugged wilderness of the place I was fortunate enough to see, even if just for a little while.

2

The next morning, after we'd settled into our cabins and got a feel for the ship, we set out for Tracy Arm Fjord. I could feel a quiet thrill running through me as we sailed out of the harbor, the ship cutting through the smooth, dark water as mountains rose on either side of us, tall and imposing. The air was crisp, tinged with salt and the fresh bite of glacial wind.

Cassie, Sarah, and I found a spot near the edge of the deck with some chairs and a small table, bundled up in blankets we'd pulled from the cabin. The sky was clouded but bright, and the landscape was so beautiful it barely felt real.

Not long after we'd settled in, Jack came around with a tray of drinks. He gave me a quick, warm smile as he handed me a glass of what looked like a summery cocktail, an amber-colored drink with a sprig of mint floating on top.

"Thought you might like something to match the scenery," he said, his eyes glinting as he handed the drink to me.

"Thanks," I replied, catching his gaze for just a beat longer than I'd meant to. "What's in it?"

"It's an Alaskan twist on a whiskey smash. Local honey and some wild mint I got from the last port. You'll have to tell me if it holds up to the view." His tone was playful, teasing, and I felt my cheeks warm a little in the cold air.

"Oh, it's definitely a high bar," I said, raising the glass to my lips and taking a sip. The drink was smooth, sweet, and slightly smoky, a perfect mix of flavors that tasted like the mountains themselves.

Jack lingered by our group, chatting easily with Cassie and Sarah, who were more than happy to grill him on all the ins and outs of life as a bartender on a boat. He answered with stories about the unique characters he'd met over the years, from solo travelers seeking solitude to eccentric millionaires.

But every once in a while, his gaze would slide back to me, and there was a spark there that made my heart beat just a little faster. At one point, he leaned in, close enough that I could feel the warmth of him even through the chill of the air.

"So, Mackenzie," he said, lowering his voice slightly. "What brings you all the way out here to Alaska?"

I paused, considering how to answer. "Adventure," I said finally, feeling a bit bold. "And maybe... a little bit of getting away from the familiar."

He nodded, his eyes never leaving mine. "Well, you've come to the right place," he said, a hint of something knowing in his voice. "Alaska has a way of getting under your skin."

Our conversation dipped and wove, going from light-hearted topics about the ship to deeper questions about what had drawn each of us to Alaska. It was easy to get lost in talking to him—he had this quiet confidence and seemed genuinely interested in what I had to say, asking questions that made me pause and really think about my answers. It felt like a refreshing change from the small talk back home, where everything seemed so predictable.

Cassie nudged me at one point, her eyebrow raised with a smirk as she caught on to our exchange. She'd seen me flirt before, sure, but there was something different about the way Jack looked at me, like he saw through all the little barriers I didn't even realize I'd put up. She shot me a knowing look, but I brushed her off, hoping she wouldn't say anything to embarrass me.

Later, as the sun began to sink and the fjord's cliffs rose up around us, the sky turned a deep blue, almost violet. The deck lights blinked on, casting a warm glow over everything. Jack returned with another round of drinks, this time handing me a mug of something steaming and spicy that smelled like cinnamon and cloves.

"Here," he said, handing it to me. "For when the sun goes down and it gets colder."

"Thanks," I said softly, feeling a strange warmth settle over me that had nothing to do with the drink.

As I took a sip, I noticed his gaze lingering, his smile a little softer than before. We watched each other in comfortable silence, both of us leaning against the railing as we looked out at the water, which shimmered faintly under the dimming light.

"It's beautiful out here," I murmured, more to myself than to him.

"It really is," he agreed, his voice low. But when I turned, I caught him looking at me, and I got the feeling he wasn't just talking about the fjord.

Just then, the boat passed a small iceberg, its jagged edges glowing a pale blue under the darkening sky. Cassie and Sarah called me over to see, and I gave Jack one last smile before walking back toward my friends, my heart light and fluttery in my chest.

* * *

The next morning, we woke early, bundled in layers, and took to the kayaks after anchoring near the mouth of Tracy Arm. The water was a deep, steel-blue, stretching out in every direction like a glassy mirror, and every so often, small icebergs floated past, their edges tinged with an icy blue glow. My heart beat faster as we paddled out, slipping through the chilly air that seemed to amplify every sound—the creak of our paddles, the echo of a bird calling from the cliffs above, the gentle splash of the water against the kayak hulls.

Jack was our guide again, paddling in the kayak beside me. The two of us were slightly ahead of Cassie and Sarah, who lingered a few paces behind, taking photos and excitedly pointing at every passing iceberg. Jack glanced over at me with a warm smile as we drifted around a cluster of small, crystal-blue icebergs.

"Bet you don't see this back home," he teased, his paddle slicing effortlessly through the water.

"Not even close," I said, laughing. "I think my biggest adventure lately was getting my car out of a snowbank last winter."

He chuckled, his gaze moving back to the water. "Well, I think you've traded up for something a little more scenic."

We drifted in silence for a few moments, both of us staring out at the incredible landscape around us. The fjord's cliffs loomed high, and waterfalls cascaded down their dark rock faces, the sound lost in the vastness of it all. Suddenly, a low, rumbling sound broke the stillness. Jack looked up, pointing ahead. "Listen. That's the glacier."

I followed his gaze to a massive wall of ice at the far end of the fjord. It rose up in a jagged, towering cliff, glowing in shades of icy blue and white. Even from this distance, I could feel the sheer power of it, like nature's monument to itself.

As we paddled closer, I noticed several sea lions resting on an iceberg, their sleek, wet bodies stretched out and glistening under the soft light. One of them lifted its head lazily, as if slightly annoyed by the disturbance, before going back to sleep.

"Wow," I whispered, trying not to make too much noise as I took in the scene. The sea lions looked so peaceful and at ease, their shapes contrasting sharply with the harsh edges of the ice.

Jack gave a small smile. "They know all the good spots around here. Warmer up there, believe it or not. The ice keeps the sun's heat longer than the water."

I raised an eyebrow. "Didn't take you for a sea lion expert."

He shrugged, grinning. "I've picked up a thing or two working out here."

We lingered in that spot, watching the sea lions and listening to the sounds of the fjord. The peace of it all was almost surreal, the silence deep and soothing. Then, a loud cracking sound echoed across the fjord as a piece of the glacier calved, sending chunks of ice tumbling down with a thunderous roar into the water below. A cold mist spread out over the fjord, and Jack and I exchanged a wide-eyed look, both of us caught in the awe of the moment.

Cassie and Sarah paddled closer, their expressions mirroring my own awe. "Mack, did you see that?" Cassie gasped, her voice a mix of exhilaration and disbelief.

"Incredible," I murmured, still staring at the glacier.

After a while, we began to paddle back toward the boat, winding our way through clusters of icebergs, each one an impossible shade of blue that glowed in the faint sunlight. The air was cool, but it didn't bother me; everything felt so alive, like I was finally in sync with the natural world around me. Jack paddled close by, our boats almost touching, and for a moment, we just looked at each other, sharing the quietness and the power of the place.

"Thanks for being here," he said softly, almost as if he were speaking to the fjord itself.

I met his gaze, my heart lifting a little. "Thanks for sharing it with me."

As we reached the ship again, I felt a mix of emotions—excitement, peace, and something else I couldn't quite put a name to. But I knew one thing for sure: this place, and this moment, would stay with me forever.

* * *

Back on the boat after our unforgettable kayak trip through the fjord, we warmed up in our cozy cabin and changed out of our damp clothes, our cheeks still flushed from the cold and excitement. The crew had prepared a warm, hearty dinner for us in the dining area—a spread of freshly baked bread, seafood chowder, and salmon with roasted vegetables. The smell alone was enough to make my stomach rumble, and we eagerly found a spot at a table by the window, still watching the slowly darkening fjord.

Cassie grinned, her eyes glinting with mischief as she ladled some chowder into her bowl. "So... Jack, huh?"

I shot her a warning look, feeling the flush of embarrassment creep up my neck. "Oh, come on," I said, rolling my eyes. "It's not like that."

"Right," Sarah interjected, arching an eyebrow. "Because we definitely didn't see you two paddling around like you were the only people in the fjord." She nudged me playfully. "Mackenzie and Jack, the explorers of the Alaskan wilderness."

I felt my face grow even warmer, trying to focus on my bowl of soup as I attempted to laugh it off. "We were just chatting," I said, feigning nonchalance. "I mean, he's friendly with all the guests. It's his job."

Cassie didn't buy it for a second, her expression only more amused as she leaned in, lowering her voice to a conspiratorial whisper. "He's cute, Mackenzie. Like, really cute. And he's definitely got a thing for you."

I opened my mouth to argue, but... I couldn't deny it, at least not to myself. There was something about Jack's easy confidence, the way he seemed so at home in this rugged, wild setting. And the way he'd looked at me today while we were paddling around the icebergs—something about it had felt electric. Still, I shrugged, not wanting to give them any ammunition. "He's probably like that with everyone," I insisted, poking at my bread to avoid their gazes.

"Oh, come on," Sarah said with a smirk. "He didn't seem like he was watching everyone out on that fjord. In fact, I think he spent more time looking at you than at the actual glacier."

I couldn't help laughing then, my defenses crumbling. "Maybe... I mean, he's a nice guy. And, okay, fine—yes, he's cute."

Cassie grinned triumphantly, holding up her glass of wine. "That's all I needed to hear. Here's to Alaska's finest tour guide!"

We all laughed and clinked glasses, our spirits high from the day's adventures. The conversation drifted to other things—work, life back home. Cassie and Sarah shared their grumbles about office politics and the deadlines waiting for them, while I talked about my own writing deadlines, the half-finished stories gathering dust on my laptop.

"It's nice to get away from it all, though," I said with a sigh, letting myself sink back into my chair. "No emails, no deadlines... just the ocean and mountains."

Sarah nodded, her expression softening. "Yeah, you really needed this. And, who knows, maybe you'll come back from this trip with more than just travel stories. A certain Alaskan bartender, maybe?"

"Sarah!" I laughed, exasperated, though secretly, I was grateful for the lighthearted ribbing. It made everything feel a little less complicated.

Cassie, though, wasn't done. She gave me a playful nudge. "Oh, come on, Mackenzie. I saw that look you gave him on the kayak. And, look, I think he's great for you—cute, adventurous, and he lives in Alaska! Maybe he's exactly what you need."

"Alright, alright," I said, laughing. "Maybe I'm... considering it. But let's not get carried away, okay?"

The girls just grinned knowingly, as though they'd already won some kind of unspoken battle. I tried to pretend like it was all just silly talk, but as I looked out the window at the vast, quiet water, I felt that tiny flicker of possibility in my chest.

* * *

That night, after a long day of adventure and laughter, I retreated to my cabin, the gentle sway of the boat lulling me into a sense of tranquility. I pushed open the small window and let the cool ocean air wash over me, bringing with it the salty scent of the sea.

I stood there, gazing out at the expanse of water that stretched to the horizon, shimmering under the moonlight. The moon hung low, a bright orb illuminating the waves, each crest glimmering like scattered diamonds against the deep blue canvas of the ocean. It was mesmerizing, almost surreal, as the silvery light danced on the surface, reflecting in a way that made the water appear alive.

The sound of the waves was soothing, a rhythmic pulse that wrapped around me like a comforting blanket. Each crash against the boat created a symphony of soft roars and whispers, reminding me of the vastness of the world beyond my worries and responsibilities back home.

As I leaned against the window frame, I thought about the day— It all felt like a dream, and yet, here I was, enveloped in the beauty of it all.

I couldn't help but smile, feeling a sense of peace settle over me. My heart raced a little as I thought of Jack—the way he'd looked at me earlier, the laughter we shared, and the connection that felt electric every time we were close. The moonlight danced in my chest, too, warming my thoughts as I recalled the easy banter we'd exchanged, the playful teasing that felt so natural between us.

I sighed softly, the sound swallowed by the waves outside. There was something special about this trip—something that stirred within me, a sense of possibility and adventure. I could feel it in my bones, like the rhythm of the ocean urging me to embrace the moment.

But even as I savored the beauty around me, I couldn't help but wonder about what lay ahead. The quiet of the cabin wrapped around me, and I let my mind drift. Would this trip change everything? Would I allow myself to pursue whatever this feeling was with Jack?

With the sound of the waves serenading me and the moon watching over, I closed my eyes for a moment, letting myself imagine a future where I could have both adventure and connection—where I could chase my dreams and still find someone who made me feel alive.

As the boat rocked gently beneath me, I knew one thing for certain: I wasn't ready for this adventure to end, not soon, not ever.

3

The next morning, we set off for Hoonah, a tiny town West of Juneau, making our way through the fjords as the early light poured over the still, glacial waters. I leaned against the ship's railing, sipping coffee and soaking in the view, grateful for the peaceful start to the day. Cassie and Sarah joined me, their eyes wide and appreciative as the landscape seemed to stretch endlessly around us.

Jack was up early, too, taking care of last-minute preparations and making sure everyone on board was comfortable. Every now and then, he'd look over and give me a nod or a small smile, sending that familiar flicker of excitement through me.

"We're in for a treat today, ladies," Jack announced, his voice carrying over the quiet murmur of the water. "We're heading back toward Juneau, and this area is prime territory for humpback whales. So keep your eyes peeled."

At his words, a ripple of excitement passed through the group as everyone grabbed their cameras and binoculars, ready to catch a glimpse of the whales. Jack joined us at the railing, pointing out where we might spot them surfacing, and giving us a rundown on the different species we might see.

It wasn't long before someone let out a gasp, and Jack pointed excitedly. "Over there!"

All eyes turned toward the spot, and sure enough, a massive tail lifted from the water before disappearing again with a splash. Everyone cheered, thrilled at the sight, and my heart raced as I leaned out for a better view.

We watched, captivated, as more whales began to surface. Sometimes it was just a faint ripple or a small, barely-there blow from a spout. Other times, a massive tail would breach the water and splash back down, sending waves across the surface. The sheer size of these creatures left us all in awe, and I couldn't help feeling humbled, standing there with the Alaskan wilderness spread out around us, these giants gliding through the ocean below.

"They're incredible, aren't they?" Jack's voice was close beside me, soft enough that it felt like our own private moment.

I nodded, hardly able to take my eyes off the water. "They really are. I feel like I'm in one of those nature documentaries, like I can't believe I'm seeing this with my own eyes."

He chuckled. "It never gets old. People think Alaska is all snow and ice, but there's so much life here if you know where to look."

I stole a glance at him, feeling that familiar warmth spread through me. There was something about seeing Jack out here, completely in his element, that made him even more magnetic. He leaned over the railing beside me, watching the water intently, and I couldn't help but admire his quiet appreciation for the place he called home.

Suddenly, there was another splash, and a mother humpback breached with her calf close behind, their massive bodies arching through the water. The group gasped in unison, and someone clapped with delight.

"That's her calf," Jack explained, his eyes lighting up as he shared in our excitement. "They're teaching the little one to breach—it's a way for them to communicate, and sometimes it's just for fun."

Sarah squeezed my arm, her face beaming. "This is incredible! Mackenzie, I'm so glad you talked us into this trip."

I laughed, still mesmerized by the whales. "Me too. It's worth every freezing moment."

Cassie leaned over, taking a video with her phone. "I've never seen anything like this. Alaska's magic, seriously."

We watched for a while longer, the whales putting on a show that felt like it was just for us. When the last tail disappeared beneath the waves, we all lingered at the railing, watching the water as if waiting for an encore.

Jack stepped away to check on the rest of the passengers, but not before sending me a quick smile. "Looks like you picked the perfect week to come out here," he said, his eyes lingering on mine for a moment. Then he turned to help another guest, and I was left smiling into my coffee, feeling the gentle sway of the boat and the afterglow of the incredible experience we'd just witnessed.

As we started to pull into Hoonah, the memory of the whales still fresh in our minds, I couldn't shake the feeling that this trip was going to be even more life-changing than I'd imagined.

* * *

We arrived in Hoonah with the sun high overhead, casting a golden glow on the quaint, picturesque town. Small wooden houses dotted the shoreline, and fishing boats rocked gently in the harbor. Hoonah had the charm of a place untouched by time, and stepping off the boat, I immediately felt as if we'd stumbled into a cozy Alaskan postcard.

Cassie and Sarah were already buzzing with excitement, their eyes darting to the shops, the docks, and the lush green mountain looming in the distance.

"Okay, where to first?" Cassie asked, practically bouncing on her toes.

"We definitely have to do the zipline," I said, feeling a surge of both excitement and nerves. "I read that it's the longest and fastest in North America."

Sarah's eyes widened. "Longest and fastest? Are we sure this is a good idea?"

Cassie grinned, nudging her. "Come on, where's your sense of adventure?"

After a little wandering through the charming streets, we made our way to the zipline loading area. We joined a small group of tourists waiting for their turn before spending an hour or so on a bus winding up through the mountains to get to the zipline. Cassie and Sarah exchanged glances, their excitement catching on as they watched others glide down the zipline with shouts of exhilaration echoing through the trees.

When it was finally our turn, a guide helped me climb into the basket-like harness and clip into the line. The platform stretched out over the treetops, and from this height, I could see all of Hoonah below us—the docks, the winding roads, and even the yacht over by the docks. My heart pounded as I peeked over the edge, adrenaline making my hands a little shaky.

Cassie gave me a thumbs-up, her face filled with determination. "Ready?"

"Ready as I'll ever be," I replied, trying to sound braver than I felt.

Before I could think too much about it, the guide counted down, and with a click, I was launched off the platform. The wind whipped around me as I sped down the line, soaring over the lush canopy below. My fear melted into exhilaration, and I couldn't help but laugh, the sound lost in the rush of the wind. The view was breathtaking—endless trees, mountains, and the deep blue of the ocean stretching to the horizon.

When I reached the other end and touched down on the platform, I was still grinning, adrenaline making my cheeks flush.

"That was incredible!" I shouted as Cassie and Sarah zipped down after me, their screams of joy echoing through the trees. They landed beside me, both beaming and out of breath.

"I want to do it again," Sarah said, a little breathless as she unbuckled her harness.

Cassie laughed, nodding in agreement. "Same! But maybe after I catch my breath."

As we explored, the quiet charm of Hoonah settled around us, and I felt grateful for this little break from the world. The simple beauty of the town and the thrill of the zipline had made it a perfect day, one I knew I'd remember long after we left Alaska.

Before heading back to the boat, we stopped at a lookout point overlooking the ocean, taking a moment to soak in the view and the sense of peace that only Alaska seemed able to provide.

"This place is amazing," Cassie said, her voice soft as she gazed out over the horizon.

I nodded, feeling a strange sense of contentment settle over me. "I think I could stay here forever."

Our next stop was to the local grocery store. We had heard rumors of the exorbitant prices, but nothing could prepare us for what we saw. Everything was at least two or three times more expensive than what we were used to. After speaking with a local man, I was told that most locals take the ferry to Juneau once a month to stock up on groceries and only purchase things here if they absolutely needed to.

I couldn't imagine what it must be like for them to be so disconnected from the rest of the world, to live a completely different lifestyle than what I was used to. It seemed lonely, yet freeing at the same time.

With the sun beginning to dip toward the mountains, we made our way back to the boat, each of us carrying a little piece of Hoonah's magic with us. As we climbed aboard, I couldn't help but glance back, already missing the tranquility of the tiny town tucked between the ocean and the wilderness.

* * *

Back on the boat, I found Jack cleaning up behind the bar as the evening lights cast a warm glow around the deck. He looked up when he saw us boarding and gave a little wave, his easy smile making me feel instantly at home.

"Hey, how was Hoonah?" he called, wiping his hands on a towel as I made my way over.

"It was amazing!" I grinned, practically bursting to share every detail. "We went ziplining, which was terrifying and exhilarating. And we wandered through the shops, saw some amazing views, and just... I don't know. There's something really peaceful about that place."

He chuckled, leaning on the counter. "You went on *that* zipline? I thought it was a rite of passage to be terrified of it."

"Hey, I survived!" I replied, raising my hands in mock protest. "And it was worth it. I'll admit, though, I screamed the whole way down."

He laughed, his blue eyes crinkling with amusement. "I bet you did. So, did you bring me back any souvenirs?"

I smirked, pulling out a small carved bear I'd impulsively picked up at one of the shops. It was rough and handmade, probably a little silly, but I handed it over with a dramatic flourish. "For you. A symbol of Alaskan bravery."

Jack raised his eyebrows, taking the bear and examining it with exaggerated seriousness. "I'll cherish this forever," he said, his tone playfully solemn. "It'll sit proudly here at the bar as a reminder of your bravery."

We both laughed, and I felt a warmth spread through me that had nothing to do with the evening chill. Cassie and Sarah disappeared below deck, but I lingered, settling onto a stool at the bar.

"Want to hang out for a bit?" he asked, tilting his head toward the cozy area of couches by the windows. "I was just about to wrap up for the night."

"Sounds good to me," I replied, trying to keep my voice casual.

Jack poured us each a drink—something warm and a little spicy—and we made our way to the couches. As we sat down, he pulled out a deck of cards from a drawer nearby and started shuffling them.

"Ever played Texas hold'em?" he asked, giving me a teasing glance as he dealt the cards.

I shook my head. "You might have to teach me. And don't think you're off the hook; I still have about a million Hoonah stories to tell you."

"Deal," he said, smiling as he dealt our hands. "I'm all ears."

For the next couple of hours, we traded stories, laughed, and slowly, I learned the ropes of Texas hold'em. Turns out, he was pretty competitive—or maybe he was just pretending to be, since he seemed to find endless amusement in pointing out every time I made a strategic "blunder."

"You're terrible at hiding your cards," he laughed at one point, leaning a little closer. "It's like you want me to see your hand."

"Or maybe it's my secret strategy," I replied with a grin, raising an eyebrow. "Ever think of that?"

"Oh, really?" His face was only inches from mine, his eyes bright with playful challenge. I felt my pulse skip a little, suddenly very aware of the nearness between us.

"Yep. I call it... reverse psychology." I laughed, trying to sound nonchalant but feeling a flush creep over my cheeks. I dropped my gaze to the cards, trying to refocus, but every time I looked back up, he was looking right at me, a small smile playing on his lips.

"So tell me, brave zipline survivor," he said, his voice softening just a bit, "what's your next big adventure?"

"Oh, who knows?" I shrugged, trying to sound lighthearted. "Back to reality, I guess. Writing deadlines, New York, city chaos." I glanced out the window, seeing the moonlit waves reflecting off the water. "But I'd take more of this if I could."

"Maybe you can," he said, his gaze steady. "This doesn't have to be just a once-in-a-lifetime trip, you know."

For a moment, the words hung between us, soft and unspoken, as if he was offering something more than just the idea of another Alaskan adventure.

"I'll keep that in mind," I said softly, feeling a flutter in my chest that wasn't from the gin. I met his eyes again, the hint of a smile on my lips.

We continued playing, talking quietly, our words mingling with the soft sounds of the boat creaking gently on the water. Eventually, my hand landed on his for just a moment as we reached for the cards at the same time, and a warm buzz shot through me.

"It's getting late," he said eventually, though he didn't seem in any hurry to go anywhere.

"Yeah," I replied reluctantly, barely hiding the disappointment in my voice.

But as we packed up the cards and lingered for a moment longer, I couldn't shake the feeling that this evening—this easy, quiet time spent together—was something I'd be thinking about long after we left Alaska.

4

The next day, the skies were dark and heavy, with rain splattering against the windows of the boat as we made our way toward Sitka. I'd been looking forward to watching the scenery from the deck, but the steady drizzle kept everyone inside, tucked away with books or chatting in the cozy common room. After breakfast, I wandered over to the bar area where Jack was organizing bottles and restocking supplies, his usual easy smile brightening up the rainy morning.

"Guess there's no escaping the rain today," I said, pulling up a seat.

Jack looked up and grinned. "Welcome to Alaska in the summer. It's just part of the charm, right?"

"Sure," I laughed, "if 'charm' means soaking wet and shivering."

"Hey, it's all about perspective." He shrugged, finishing his work and sliding a hot cup of tea across the bar toward me. "You wanted the real Alaskan experience, right? Rain's just part of the deal."

I wrapped my hands around the warm cup, taking a sip, and letting the heat spread through me. "Guess I'm getting my money's worth then."

He chuckled and sat down across from me. For a moment, we just sipped our drinks in comfortable silence, listening to the gentle hum of the boat and the soft patter of rain. The window beside us was fogged up, blurring the gray landscape outside. But somehow, sitting here, everything felt warm and a little magical.

"So," he said, breaking the silence, "what do you usually write about? I've been dying to ask since you mentioned you were a writer."

I shrugged, a little self-conscious. "It varies. Mostly travel pieces, stories about unique places, sometimes a bit of lifestyle stuff. I guess it's my way of exploring the world and sharing it with people, even when I'm not traveling myself."

"That's cool," he said, genuinely interested. "What's the most memorable place you've written about?"

"Hmm..." I thought for a moment. "There was this little village in Italy—hardly anyone knows about it, but it's tucked away on the coast, just stunning. I spent a few weeks there, getting to know the locals, learning about the old legends and traditions. It was one of those places that just stays with you, you know?"

Jack nodded thoughtfully. "Sounds amazing. So, does that make Alaska your next big story?"

"I hope so," I said, glancing out the window at the misty landscape. "But honestly, I didn't come here to write. This trip was more of an escape."

"Escape?" he asked, a hint of curiosity in his eyes.

"Yeah," I admitted, feeling a little embarrassed. "I guess I just needed a break—from the deadlines, the noise, and the... I don't know, the busyness of everything back home. Alaska seemed like the perfect place to just... breathe."

Jack nodded slowly, and for a moment, his gaze softened, like he understood completely. "Well, I hope it's working," he said quietly. "Seems like the peace and quiet is doing you some good."

I smiled, feeling a warmth spread through me that had nothing to do with the tea. "It is," I replied softly. "Especially with good company."

He raised his cup in a playful toast. "To new adventures."

We clinked our mugs together, both of us smiling in a way that made the boat, the rain, and everything else fade into the background. The hours drifted by as we shared stories—me talking about some of my favorite travel memories, him recounting tales from his time working on the boat, from wild storms to the best (and strangest) passengers he'd met over the years. As the day wore on, it felt like I'd known him forever.

In the afternoon, when the rain showed no sign of letting up, Jack suggested a game of Scrabble from the boat's small collection of board games. Soon, we were deep in a competitive match, with me trying to outdo his extensive knowledge of rare words.

"'Qi' is totally cheating," I protested, laughing as he tallied his points with a satisfied grin.

"It's all part of the strategy," he replied, looking entirely too pleased with himself.

By the time dinnertime rolled around, my cheeks ached from smiling and laughing. As everyone gathered in the dining area, I found myself stealing glances at Jack from across the room, feeling a growing sense of anticipation every time our eyes met.

When dinner was over, I lingered behind to help him clear the plates, savoring these last quiet moments with him before everyone else settled back into the common room.

"You know," he said softly as we stacked dishes together, "today's been one of the best days I've had in a while. Rain and all."

I looked up at him, caught off guard by the sincerity in his voice. "Me too," I admitted, feeling my heart thud a little harder.

For a moment, we just stood there, the space between us small and electric. He looked like he wanted to say something else, but instead, he simply smiled, a warmth in his eyes that I felt all the way to my core.

And as the boat gently rocked on the rainy Alaskan sea, I felt something shift, a quiet certainty settling into place.

* * *

After a peaceful evening alone in my cabin, I joined the girls back in the main lounge area. They had already gathered on the plush sectional, comfortably sprawled out with blankets and glasses of wine in hand, the remains of a charcuterie board spread out on the low table in front of them.

"Finally!" Cassie exclaimed, patting the empty cushion next to her. "We were starting to think you'd gone overboard."

"Or met up with a certain someone," Sarah added with a wink. I rolled my eyes, hiding a grin as I took a seat.

"Sorry, no exciting tales to tell—just needed a little quiet time." I wrapped myself in one of the fluffy blankets and took the glass of wine Cassie handed me. The lounge was warm and cozy, the low hum of the boat's engine blending with the sounds of gentle laughter and chatter. The girls and I settled into our usual rhythm of conversation, sharing stories and catching up on little things we hadn't had time to talk about back home.

Cassie stretched out and sighed, her expression blissful. "Is it just me, or is this the most relaxed we've felt in months?"

"It's definitely not just you," Sarah said, pulling the blanket tighter around herself. "I don't think I've fully relaxed like this since...forever, honestly. Just us, the ocean, a little wine..."

"And the scenery," I chimed in. "Nothing like the Alaskan coast to make everything else feel like it's a thousand miles away."

We clinked our glasses, a silent toast to the escape this trip was giving us. The conversation drifted, flowing from stories of old memories to updates on work and life.

"So, Mack," Cassie began, her tone teasing, "since we're all catching up... care to share what's going on with our favorite bartender?"

I shook my head, smiling despite myself. "There's nothing to share."

"Please," Sarah rolled her eyes. "You've been all smiles since you got back from your little chat with him. Admit it—you like him."

I felt a blush creeping into my cheeks. "Okay, fine. Maybe he's... nice. But it's not like anything's going to happen. We're here for only about two weeks, and then we all go back to real life."

"Doesn't mean you can't enjoy a little harmless fun while we're here," Cassie pointed out. "He's obviously into you. Everyone sees it."

"Maybe," I said, laughing a little. "But... I don't know. I don't want things to get complicated."

"Complicated is your thing, Mackenzie," Sarah joked, nudging me with her elbow. "Besides, what's life without a little adventure?"

I was about to protest again, but Cassie shushed us, pointing at the screen. "Quiet, quiet! The movie's starting."

She'd queued up a classic rom-com, and within minutes, we were laughing, sipping our wine, and letting ourselves get completely wrapped up in the charmingly unrealistic world of the movie. It felt like old times, like the high school sleepovers we used to have, where we'd stay up talking and giggling until we all fell asleep in a tangle of blankets and pillows.

We stayed there long after the movie ended, the glow from the screen casting a soft light around the room. The girls' laughter, the gentle rocking of the boat, and the warmth of the moment filled me with a sense of calm and contentment. It was a rare, perfect moment, and I knew I'd hold on to it for a long time, long after we returned home and life resumed its regular pace.

As the night grew late, we each drifted off to our cabins, my heart full and my mind lingering on thoughts of Jack.

That night, I drifted into sleep, warmth from the cozy evening with my friends still wrapped around me. My mind wandered, settling into a dream that felt so vivid it was hard to believe it wasn't real.

I was back on the boat, but instead of being with the girls, I was alone on the deck, leaning over the railing to watch the ocean. The sky was clear, starlit, and I could feel the soft night breeze on my face. It was serene—just the sound of gentle waves lapping against the hull. Then, footsteps approached from behind me, and I knew it was Jack.

"Couldn't sleep?" he asked, his voice low and familiar, carrying that easy warmth I'd come to recognize.

I turned, smiling up at him. "Just wanted some fresh air. I didn't expect anyone else to be awake."

He stepped closer, his blue eyes catching the reflection of the starlight. "Guess I'm not just anyone, then."

My breath caught, and before I could respond, he closed the distance between us. His hand brushed my cheek, warm and gentle, as he tilted my face up toward his. Everything around us felt suspended, like the night was holding its breath.

"You know, I've wanted to do this since the day I met you," he murmured, his thumb brushing across my cheek.

I didn't have time to overthink it, to analyze every word and gesture like I usually would. Instead, I just felt—warmth, anticipation, that electric pull between us. When he leaned in, his lips brushed against mine, softly at first, then more sure, deepening as if he were afraid to let the moment go.

In the dream, the kiss felt like it lasted forever, and yet not nearly long enough. He pulled back just slightly, his forehead resting against mine.

"Stay with me," he whispered, his voice barely a breath. "Don't let this be just a dream."

I opened my mouth to answer, to say something that felt right, something I'd wanted to say for longer than I'd even realized—but just then, the sky started to dim, the stars fading as though someone were dimming the lights on a stage.

The next moment, I woke up, the dream slipping from my mind like sand through my fingers. I was left lying in the darkness of my cabin, my heart still beating fast, my lips tingling with the memory of his kiss. It was hard to shake the feeling, as if a part of me had crossed a line I couldn't uncross.

I sat up, trying to gather my thoughts, my breath, feeling more awake than I had in days. It had only been a dream, but it didn't feel that way.

* * *

I woke up with a start, my heart still beating from the dream. For a few moments, I lay there, staring up at the ceiling, letting the warmth of it settle over me. Jack's face lingered in my mind—the way he'd looked at me, the feeling of his hand on my cheek. It was hard to shake the feeling that I'd actually been there with him, as if the dream had blurred with reality.

Shaking myself awake, I climbed out of bed and made my way to the small bathroom to splash some water on my face. The coolness snapped me back, and I took a few deep breaths, feeling more grounded but still a little dazed.

Outside the porthole, soft light filtered over the water. We were moving into Sitka, and through the glass, I could see a landscape dotted with trees and mist-covered mountains coming into view. It was breathtaking, almost surreal—a perfect blend of lush greenery and towering, snow-dusted peaks. I found myself mesmerized, leaning closer to the window as if I could drink it all in.

After a few minutes, I finally tore myself away and threw on jeans, a sweater, and a warm jacket, knowing the air would be chilly. The girls and I had talked about exploring Sitka today, and I was ready to get out and see more of this place that already felt so wild and different from anywhere I'd been.

I headed out to the deck, hoping to catch the sunrise over the town as we pulled closer to shore. There were a few other passengers up, bundled in coats, hands wrapped around cups of coffee, their faces lit with that same sense of awe I felt. I stepped over to the railing, pulling my jacket tighter, and looked out as the harbor came into view.

"Good morning, early riser," a voice said from behind me.

I turned to see Jack walking over, a steaming cup of coffee in each hand. He handed one to me with a slight smile, his eyes crinkling at the corners in that way that made him look so approachable, so completely himself.

"Morning," I replied, accepting the cup gratefully. "Thanks." I wrapped my hands around the mug, letting the warmth seep into my palms as I took a sip. The rich, earthy taste was a comfort against the brisk air.

"Did you sleep well?" he asked, leaning against the railing beside me, his gaze on the shoreline.

I hesitated, the remnants of my dream fluttering back, and then gave a quick nod. "Yeah, pretty well," I said, deciding to leave out the details. "Excited to see Sitka?"

"Absolutely," he replied. "It's one of my favorite spots along the Inside Passage. You're going to love it."

We stood in companionable silence for a while, watching as the boat moved steadily into the harbor. The town of Sitka unfolded before us, a charming mix of historic buildings, fishing boats lined up along the docks, and a few shops and cafes just starting to open their doors for the day. Mist lingered over the mountains, creating an ethereal feel as the sunlight slowly began to break through.

"This place is incredible," I murmured, almost to myself.

"Alaska has a way of doing that," Jack replied softly. I could feel his gaze shift toward me, but I kept my eyes on the view, my heart doing an odd little flip.

As the boat docked, the girls appeared one by one, and soon enough, our little group was ready to explore. We planned to start with breakfast in town, then wander around, take in the sights, and maybe even visit the Russian bishop's house and the nearby totem park.

With one last look at the water, I took a deep breath and followed everyone down the gangplank. I tried to push aside the lingering thoughts of my dream and focus on the day ahead, but I could still feel Jack's presence beside me, as steady and warm as the cup of coffee in my hands.

5

As soon as we stepped off the boat and onto the dock, I took a long, deep breath, savoring the crisp, pine-scented air. Sitka was different from Juneau—smaller, quieter, and somehow both more rugged and charming all at once. Mountains loomed in the distance, and the historic wooden buildings along the waterfront seemed to carry stories of their own.

"Where to first?" Cassie asked, tucking her hands into her jacket pockets as she looked around.

"I read about this amazing cafe," Sarah chimed in, already consulting her phone. "It's supposed to have the best cinnamon rolls in town."

"Lead the way!" I said with a grin, already excited to warm up with some coffee and something sweet.

We walked along the waterfront, passing locals bundled up in coats and tourists with cameras, everyone moving a bit slower, savoring the morning. Colorful fishing boats lined the docks, bobbing slightly with the movement of the water, and a few eagles circled overhead, majestic against the backdrop of snow-capped mountains. It was breathtaking.

The cafe was as quaint as promised—a cozy little place with wooden tables, windows fogged up from the warmth inside, and the smell of freshly baked goods wafting through the door. We quickly found a table by the window, where we could see the town waking up and the harbor stretching out toward the mountains.

Once our food arrived, we chatted and laughed over coffee and cinnamon rolls the size of my face, planning out the rest of the day between bites.

"We should definitely check out that Russian bishop's house," I suggested. "I read it's one of the oldest buildings here and a National Historic Landmark."

"And the totem park!" Cassie added, already on board. "I've been dying to see those totems in person."

Our morning was full of sightseeing, history, and so much laughter. We visited the Russian bishop's house, a preserved relic of Alaska's time under Russian control. Wandering through its halls felt like stepping back in time, imagining the lives that had passed through. Then we made our way to Sitka National Historical Park, where towering totem poles lined forested paths, each carved figure a unique story in wood.

As we wandered the trail, we stopped at each totem to read about its meaning and origin. The forest was peaceful, the only sounds coming from the rustling of leaves and the distant calls of eagles.

"Can you imagine living here back then?" Sarah mused as we stood in front of a particularly intricate totem.

"It would be wild," I replied, running my fingers along the smooth wood of the pole. "Just being surrounded by this wilderness, in such a small, tight-knit community... there's something magical about it."

Cassie shot me a mischievous look. "Or maybe that's just the influence of a certain someone on board the yacht."

I rolled my eyes, though I felt a blush creeping up. "It's not like that," I protested, only half-heartedly.

"Sure, sure," Sarah teased, winking. "But we can all tell there's a spark."

Ignoring their knowing looks, I led us back toward the main trail, trying to focus on the scenery rather than the fluttering in my chest. There was something about Alaska, the boat, and, yes, Jack, that made everything feel a little more alive. A little more possible.

After we finished at the totem park, we took a quick detour to the Sitka Sound Science Center, where we watched sea stars and sea urchins in touch tanks and learned about the local marine life. It was fascinating, and the whole experience left me with a renewed appreciation for just how much life there was beneath the surface of the icy waters.

By mid-afternoon, we found ourselves back near the docks. With the sun hanging low in the sky and casting a golden glow over everything, Sitka felt like something out of a storybook.

"Should we head back to the boat?" Cassie asked, glancing at me. "I'm sure you're eager to tell a certain someone all about our day."

I groaned, but I couldn't help but laugh. "You're never going to let this go, are you?"

"Not a chance," Sarah said with a grin.

As we walked back toward the yacht, I found myself feeling excited to see Jack, to share everything we'd done today. And as much as I loved exploring this town, the thought of heading back, of those quiet conversations with him, made me realize just how much this trip had already begun to change me.

* * *

The next morning, I found myself on the bow of the boat, bundled up against the early chill, watching the fog lift slowly off the water as Jack approached, holding two fishing rods and a small tackle box.

"Ready to catch your first Alaskan fish?" he asked, grinning as he held out a rod.

I took it, feeling the weight of it in my hands. "As ready as I'll ever be," I said, though I couldn't help but laugh at the slight absurdity of it. I'd never fished before, let alone in the icy waters of Alaska.

"Don't worry, it's pretty simple," Jack assured me. He came up beside me, close enough that I could feel his warmth, and placed his hands over mine, adjusting my grip. "Just hold it like this... good. Then, when you're ready, flick it forward—"

I did, a little too enthusiastically, and the line tangled at the end of the rod. I could feel my cheeks warm. "Oops," I muttered.

Jack chuckled, clearly trying to hold back his laughter. "Alright, a little less flick, a little more control," he said, reaching over to help untangle the line. "It takes some practice."

I gave it another try, this time following his instructions more carefully, and the line flew out into the water smoothly. I felt a surge of triumph. "I did it!" I said, flashing him a smile.

"Perfect," he replied, his eyes warm with encouragement. "Now we wait."

We stood there in silence, our lines drifting in the still water. The morning was calm, only the gentle rocking of the boat beneath us and the occasional call of a seagull breaking the quiet. There was something deeply relaxing about it, like all the noise and movement of daily life had just faded away.

"Are you ready to catch the biggest fish of your life?" he asked, flashing a grin that made my stomach flutter.

"Only if you can handle my competitive spirit," I teased back, leaning against the railing. "I've been known to be quite the angler."

"Oh really? You think you can out-fish me?" He raised an eyebrow, a playful challenge glimmering in his blue eyes. "You might want to lower your expectations. I've been doing this my whole life."

"Challenge accepted," I replied, crossing my arms and giving him a defiant look. "Just don't cry when I reel in the biggest catch."

He laughed, a deep sound that resonated in my chest. "We'll see about that, Miss Big Shot. But, honestly, if you want to learn a thing or two about fishing, I can teach you. I know a spot where the fish practically jump into the boat."

"Is that so?" I leaned closer, intrigued. "Tell me more about this secret fishing spot of yours."

Jack straightened, his expression turning more serious. "Well, it's not just about the spot. It's about being out on the water, you know? There's something about being surrounded by the ocean, the mountains, the whole experience. It's my dream to own my own charter fishing boat someday. To take people out, show them the beauty of Alaska, and share this passion with them."

I watched as he spoke, his enthusiasm lighting up his face. "That sounds amazing, Jack. You'd be great at it. What's stopping you?"

He hesitated for a moment, looking out at the water. "It's not easy, you know? The costs, the logistics... it takes time to get there. But I can't shake the feeling that it's what I'm meant to do. I want to create something—an experience for people to remember."

"I think you'll get there," I said, feeling a swell of admiration for his dream. "You have the passion and the skills. Plus, you've got the best teacher right here." I gestured to myself with a playful wink.

Jack laughed, his eyes sparkling with mischief. "Are you offering to be my first mate? I could use someone with your... competitive spirit."

"Absolutely! Just remember, I'm not afraid to steal the spotlight," I replied, my heart racing at the thought of spending more time with him.

"Then I better keep my fishing game strong," he shot back, stepping closer, our shoulders brushing. "Can't have you showing me up on my own boat."

The air between us crackled with energy, and I felt a blush creeping up my cheeks. I met his gaze, searching for any hint that he felt the same way.

"Maybe we should see who catches the first fish today," I suggested, trying to keep my voice steady.

Jack leaned in slightly, his expression teasing yet sincere. "You're on, but just so you know, I won't go easy on you."

"Good," I said, feeling emboldened. "I wouldn't want it any other way. So, you do this a lot?"

"Whenever I get the chance," he said, leaning back against the railing casually. "It's nice to just... slow down. I think that's one of the reasons I love working on the water. Things don't feel as rushed out here."

I nodded, watching the small ripples on the surface of the water. "I can see why. It's so different from... everything, really."

Jack turned to me, a soft smile on his face. "I'm glad you're getting a chance to experience it. A lot of people come to Alaska, see the big sights, and then leave. But there's so much more to it if you take the time."

Before I could respond, I felt a sudden tug on the line. I gasped, gripping the rod tighter. "I think I got something!"

"Alright, nice and steady," Jack coached, stepping close behind me. "Reel it in slowly, let it pull a bit, then bring it toward you."

I followed his instructions, my pulse quickening as I reeled in the line. Jack's hand came to rest on my shoulder as he guided me through it, his voice calm and steady. The fish fought hard, but with one final tug, I pulled it up and out of the water, where it dangled on the end of the line, shimmering in the morning light.

"Look at that! A nice little rockfish," Jack said proudly, giving my shoulder a squeeze. "Not bad for your first catch."

I laughed, feeling a strange sense of pride. "Guess I'm a natural," I teased, shooting him a playful grin.

Jack grinned back, his eyes glinting with something that made my stomach do a little flip. "Guess you are."

We stood there a moment, just grinning at each other, until I realized I was still holding the wriggling fish at the end of the line. "So, uh... what do I do with it now?"

He took the rod from me, carefully removing the hook and releasing the fish back into the water. "Today's a catch-and-release day," he said, watching it dart away. "No need to worry about cleaning and cooking just yet."

"Thank goodness," I said, exhaling in relief. "Though I'd probably get the hang of that, too. Maybe."

Jack laughed, tucking a stray hair behind my ear. "I don't doubt it."

We spent the rest of the morning fishing, talking in quiet voices, and watching the water stretch out endlessly around us. It was simple, and peaceful, and maybe my favorite part of the trip so far. And each time I caught him glancing at me out of the corner of his eye, a warm feeling spread through me, as if something new had started, something that felt as vast and promising as the Alaskan waters surrounding us.

"Alright, now that you've earned your fishing badge, I think it's time you help me pull up the crab pots we set out when we arrived."

A little later, after they had pulled the boat up to the spot where the crab pots were, Jack led us around to the back of the boat. He'd insisted I wear his oversized Xtratuff boots since my regular shoes wouldn't cut it on the wet deck. I slipped them on, wobbling a bit, which earned a laugh from Jack.

"Look at you," he chuckled, nodding at my clunky, over-sized feet. "Alaskan fashion suits you."

I stuck out a foot, examining the boots with mock appreciation. "I could get used to this look. These boots are almost bigger than my suitcase, though."

He grinned, handing me a pair of gloves before he walked over to the first pot. With a practiced pull, he hauled it up, water dripping as he hoisted it over the edge of the boat. Inside, a few crabs scrambled, claws clicking against the mesh as they tried to find an escape route.

I leaned closer, fascinated. "That's incredible!"

Jack raised an eyebrow, his hand hovering over the pot. "Want a closer look?"

I nodded, stepping forward, but he held up a crab with a mischievous glint in his eye, waving it near me. "You sure? They get a little nippy sometimes."

"Oh, you wouldn't dare," I warned, backing up with a laugh. But he stepped forward, the crab snapping its claws close to my arm.

"Come on, they're friendly," he teased, holding the crab closer.

"Friendly, huh?" I squealed, sidestepping him, the over-sized boots making it hard to move quickly. "You're the one who said they're 'nippy!'"

He laughed, finally lowering the crab back into the pot. "Okay, okay, I'll let you off easy." He set the pot down, pulling out a second, larger crab, and held it up carefully for me to see.

I stepped closer this time, watching the crab's claws slowly open and close. "It's strange... kind of beautiful in a way. But definitely not cute enough to be that close to my face," I said, shooting him a playful glare.

He shook his head, chuckling as he gently placed the crab back in the pot. "Fair enough. Most people aren't fans of the claws near their faces."

As he went through the pots, he explained the different types of crabs and the best ways to catch them, a casual confidence in his voice that made it clear he knew these waters inside and out. I found myself mesmerized, watching him work, comfortable and focused, the ocean stretching behind him. The salty air and sound of the waves made it feel like we were the only two people in the world.

After a few more pulls, he set the last pot down and wiped his hands on a towel, giving me a sly grin. "Well, that wasn't so scary, was it?"

I looked down at the boots, which felt even heavier now. "Maybe a little," I admitted, laughing as I clomped my way back around to the front deck, leaving the faintest, wet footprints behind.

* * *

Later that evening, the dining room on the boat was filled with the aroma of fresh crab, steamed to perfection. Jack had cracked open the first few for us, making sure we didn't struggle, and there was plenty of melted butter and lemon to go around. We dug in, everyone exchanging glances of pure bliss with each bite.

"This is amazing," I sighed, savoring the tender, sweet flavor of the crab. "I don't think I can go back to the frozen stuff after this."

Jack chuckled from his spot at the head of the table. "That's the point. Fresh off the boat's the only way to go."

Once everyone had their fill, the conversation lulled, and Jack excused himself to clean up in the kitchen. My friends took the opportunity to pounce.

"So, Mackenzie," Cassie leaned over, raising a brow as she dipped another crab leg in butter. "You and Jack seem... cozy."

The other girls murmured in agreement, leaning in with eager expressions. My cheeks grew warm under their scrutiny.

"I mean," I started, trying to sound casual, "he's been... nice to me."

"Oh, please," Sarah smirked. "You're blushing like crazy, Mack. It's more than that."

I put my fork down, the weight of their stares pushing me toward honesty. "Fine. Maybe it is a little more than that."

Cassie's eyes lit up, a grin spreading across her face. "Knew it! So... what's going on with you two?"

I glanced toward the kitchen, making sure Jack was still occupied. Then, lowering my voice, I finally confessed, "It's been unexpected, honestly. I never thought I'd meet someone like him on this trip. He's kind, funny... and knows so much about this place. There's something so grounded about him, you know? I keep catching myself thinking about what it'd be like to actually start something with him."

Sarah's mouth fell open. "Wait... are you seriously considering a long-distance thing?"

I laughed, shrugging. "That's the thing—I don't know what I'm thinking! But I feel like there's something here, something real."

"But," Cassie cut in gently, "what about your plans back home? The city, writing, all of that?"

I sighed, feeling that familiar tug. "That's why I'm conflicted. I've spent years dreaming of making it as a writer. But now... this trip, meeting Jack—it's making me question what I really want."

The girls exchanged a knowing look, as if they could already see where my heart was headed, even if I wasn't quite there yet.

"You deserve someone who makes you feel this way," Sarah said softly. "And maybe it's not about giving up your dreams... but letting them grow in a new way, you know?"

Cassie nodded. "Yeah, sometimes the best things in life are the ones you didn't plan for."

I looked down at my plate, Jack's laugh echoing from the kitchen, and realized they might be right.

6

As we set out on the journey back to Juneau, a thick layer of clouds rolled in, casting everything in soft, gray light. The waves grew choppier as we moved further into open waters, and before long, a light rain tapped on the windows, steady and calming. Jack called it "a baby storm," not enough to worry about but just enough to keep us cozy inside.

When the boat hit a particularly large swell, we felt a small lurch beneath us. Sarah stumbled, laughing, grabbing onto a nearby couch.

"Did anyone else feel that?" she giggled.

"Feel what?" Jack's voice came from the galley, where he was preparing hot chocolate for everyone.

Just then, another wave hit, and we were lifted a couple of inches off the floor, only to come back down in a gentle thud. The girls and I burst into laughter as we caught our balance.

"Let's do it on purpose!" Lila suggested, her eyes bright with excitement. "Every time the boat hits a wave, jump!"

We gathered in the middle of the room, timing our jumps with the next wave. When it lifted the boat just right, we jumped up and, for a moment, we were suspended in the air, floating as if gravity had vanished. Our laughs echoed through the room as we repeated it, catching air with each wave, like kids on a trampoline.

Jack joined us, balancing a tray of hot chocolate mugs with a grin. "You guys are crazy," he teased, watching us launch ourselves up and down with each swell.

"It's way too fun!" I said, taking my mug from him as he handed it over. "You have to try it, Jack."

He raised an eyebrow, feigning reluctance, but then the next wave hit, and he gave in, springing up and coming back down with us. For a moment, we all laughed, suspended in that simple thrill, letting the waves carry us.

Eventually, as the storm calmed, we huddled together in the lounge area, draped in blankets and sipping our hot chocolates. The rain pattered on the windows, and the dim light made the room feel like a cozy haven.

"Movie time?" Sarah suggested, flicking through the stack of DVDs. We settled on an old favorite, a rom-com that had us laughing and sighing at all the right moments. As the movie played, I found myself glancing at Jack, who had wedged himself into the seat next to mine. Our shoulders touched, a small, comforting connection, and I felt my heart do a little leap, as if it, too, was caught on a wave.

Outside, the storm had all but passed, leaving the boat rocking gently in its wake. As the final credits rolled, we lay there in peaceful silence, still caught in the feeling of that fleeting flight and the warmth of being together.

* * *

The rain had let up by the time we reached the next stretch of calm waters, leaving everything on deck misty and soft in the gray afternoon. I headed outside, eager to breathe in the fresh air and maybe catch a glimpse of something magical in the fog over the water. Jack followed, carrying two mugs of coffee. He handed me one and took a spot beside me, leaning casually against the railing.

"Thanks," I said, taking a sip and letting the warmth of the coffee cut through the cool air.

"Nice out here, huh?" he said, his voice quiet, almost as if he didn't want to disturb the peace of the moment.

"It is. It's...breathtaking." I looked out over the water, where mountains barely visible through the mist rose like shadows. "Alaska's definitely the right place for an escape."

He gave me a sideways glance, a soft smile tugging at his lips. "So, Mack—what are you escaping from?"

I raised an eyebrow, taken aback by the nickname. "Mack, huh?"

"Yeah," he shrugged, looking a bit sheepish but also confident, like he'd decided on it long ago. "Feels right. Reminds me of the fish - Mackerel. And besides, I don't think anyone else has dared to shorten your name yet in that way. Do I get points for originality?"

I laughed. "Maybe a few points. Guess I'm just not used to nicknames." I leaned on the railing beside him. "But 'Mack' or even 'Mackerel' works."

"Good. Then it's settled." He took a sip of his coffee, looking pleased with himself.

We both stared out over the water for a while, the boat gently bobbing as the mist started to lift, revealing more of the rugged landscape ahead. I could feel him watching me, the way his gaze would shift back and forth from the mountains to my face, lingering just a bit longer each time.

"So, about that escape," he said after a pause. "I mean, not to pry, but I don't take you for the usual 'escape to Alaska' type. Is it work? Something...or someone?" He gave me a teasing look, his eyes bright.

"Not a someone," I replied, smiling at his attempt to fish for details. "But work...yeah, that's part of it. I just needed a change, you know? To step away for a bit."

"I get it," he said, nodding. "I needed a change, too, back when I decided to take this gig. Alaska has a way of pulling people in and making them face things, whether they're ready or not."

His words hung in the air between us, and I felt something click, like he understood exactly what I'd been trying to escape.

"So, why Alaska for you?" I asked, turning the tables. "What were you escaping?"

He chuckled, looking away for a second. "Same thing as everyone, I guess. Life gets a little too predictable. And maybe..." He hesitated, as if debating whether to finish the thought, but he did. "Maybe I was hoping to find something different out here."

He glanced at me, his eyes warm with a hint of curiosity, and for a second, I wondered if I might just be part of the "something different" he was looking for. I smiled, feeling the blush creeping into my cheeks.

"You're good at this, you know," he said after a pause.

"Good at what?"

"Dodging questions," he teased, his voice playful. "But you're also good at...being here. Just seems like you fit, even if you say you're here to escape."

I shrugged, feeling a bit exposed under his steady gaze. "Maybe Alaska is bringing out a different side of me," I said, deflecting slightly but meaning it, too.

"Well, I like it." His voice was soft, with a hint of something more beneath it. "Mack, Alaska suits you."

"Thanks," I replied, my voice catching just a little. He was still looking at me, his gaze warm and unwavering.

The boat rocked gently, bringing us a few inches closer. For a second, I thought he might lean in, but instead, he just kept his eyes on me, like he was content to let the moment unfold naturally. And as we stood there, side by side on the deck, I couldn't help but wonder if maybe, just maybe, Alaska wasn't the only thing making me feel like I belonged.

* * *

Sitting in my cabin with my laptop open, I tried to gather my thoughts on the trip so far, hoping to focus on the travel piece I'd promised to work on. The trip had been one of discovery, each day overflowing with breathtaking sights, serene moments, and the kind of experiences I knew readers would want to devour: watching whales cresting the waves, walking along quiet shorelines, and laughing with my friends late into the night.

But I'd barely written a paragraph before my mind drifted off the page to Jack.

I groaned, leaning back in my chair. I was here to write a travel piece, not some summer romance story! But no matter how much I tried, the words about glaciers and sea lions blurred, and my thoughts drifted back to him—his easy laugh, the warm look in his eyes, the way he called me "Mack" like it was the most natural thing in the world.

I rubbed my temples, trying to pull myself together. Focus, I told myself. I typed out a few sentences about the Tracy Arm Fjord, but each line felt flat, as though the wonder had been sucked right out of it. Nothing captured the way it actually felt—like I was part of something wild and grand and deeply personal. And I had to admit, part of that feeling was Jack.

My fingers hovered over the keys, hesitating. Could I work him into the story in some subtle way? I laughed at myself—of course not. He was the reason I couldn't concentrate, not the solution. But I couldn't deny that he was part of the trip, a part I hadn't planned on but one I couldn't seem to shake.

My thoughts drifted back to earlier that day, the quiet warmth between us as we watched the mist rising from the mountains. That moment we shared on deck, when he looked at me like there was nowhere else he'd rather be, like he saw me in a way I hadn't expected...no, hadn't even dared to hope for.

I sighed, closing the laptop and letting my eyes wander out the cabin window. The soft glow of the sun had faded into an overcast afternoon, but there was still a hazy beauty in the way the light hit the water, gray and muted.

A knock at the door startled me, and I quickly shut the laptop, as if somehow Jack could see my thoughts on my face.

"Hey, Mack," Sarah's voice called softly through the door. "We're about to grab lunch—thought you might want to join us?"

"Coming!" I called back, feeling my cheeks warm.

As I slipped my shoes on, I took a deep breath, steadying myself. Maybe a break would clear my head. But as I reached for the door, I couldn't help but wonder if any amount of fresh air could shake this feeling building inside me—a quiet, constant pull toward him that felt as sure and steady as the sea outside my window.

I'd barely taken a step outside when I spotted Jack leaning against the railing, looking out over the waves. He turned, a little surprised, as I approached, but he gave me that easy, warm smile I'd started to crave more than I wanted to admit.

"Hey, Mack," he said, his voice softer than usual. "Out here for a bit of air?"

"Yeah," I answered, leaning on the railing beside him. "Thought I'd take a break from my endless attempts at writing. The ocean's much more inspiring."

Jack chuckled. "Hard to argue with that. Though I'd imagine you're inspiring enough on your own."

The words hung in the air between us, and for a moment, I couldn't breathe. His hand reached out, almost instinctively, and his fingers brushed over mine, sending a warm spark through me.

"Jack..." I began, searching for the right words, but he interrupted.

"Mackenzie, I didn't plan on...feeling this way." He ran a hand through his hair, looking almost shy, and it took me off guard. "But ever since you boarded this boat, it's been...different. You're different."

The air was thick between us as his words sank in. I bit my lip, feeling my heart pounding with a mix of excitement and worry. "I've been feeling it too, Jack," I admitted softly. "But... what do we do about it?"

He looked at me, his blue eyes steady but uncertain. "I don't know. I mean, you're not here to stay. You've got a life, a career waiting for you when you get off this boat. And I don't want to get in the way of that."

I swallowed, the weight of his words grounding me in a way I hadn't expected. "I don't want to hurt you, Jack. I've been focused on my career for so long... but this, whatever this is between us, it's real."

We stood there in silence, the only sounds the gentle lapping of waves against the hull and the quiet hum of the boat. It was a strange feeling—knowing something was real but realizing it might not have a clear path forward.

Jack took a breath, his fingers still grazing mine. "Maybe we don't have to figure it out right now," he said finally, a slight smile touching his lips. "Maybe we just... see where it goes?"

"Maybe," I whispered, nodding. It wasn't a solution, but it felt like a promise.

Our eyes met, and for a moment, it felt like the world had shrunk down to just us, just this quiet understanding that neither of us fully grasped but weren't quite ready to let go of. As long as I was on this boat, I'd take every minute I had with him, savoring each stolen glance and quiet conversation, wondering what would happen once I finally had to walk away.

* * *

The sun hung low on the horizon, casting a warm, golden light over Funter Bay as we made our way to the little hidden beach. This was one of Jack's favorite spots, and he was practically buzzing with excitement as we picked our way over the smooth, seaweed-draped rocks toward the rocky ledge. Above us, the trees leaned in, some of them growing at angles so extreme they looked ready to topple right into the water. But Jack assured me they'd been that way for years, "like natural swings."

When we reached the rocks, I saw the old buoy hanging from a thick, weather-beaten rope, swaying slightly in the breeze. It was tied to one of the leaning trees, dangling above the water in a way that seemed inviting and reckless all at once.

Jack grinned and looked at me. "Ever swung on one of these before?"

I raised an eyebrow, eyeing the buoy. "I can't say I've had the pleasure."

"Well, today's your lucky day!" He flashed a mischievous smile, and before I could argue, he was scrambling up a small outcropping of rocks next to the tree. "C'mon, climb up here with me. It's easier to jump onto the buoy from up here."

I followed, carefully placing my feet on the rough stones. Jack reached down, offering me a hand when I got close enough. His grip was strong and warm, and as he pulled me up beside him, our shoulders brushed. From this vantage point, the buoy swing looked like a challenge and an invitation.

Jack grinned as he leaned over to catch the rope. He gave it a good tug, then held it out to me. "Want to go first?"

I hesitated, feeling the weight of the rope in my hands. The swing looked sturdy enough, but something about flinging myself off a rock over chilly Alaskan water gave me pause. I shrugged the towel off my shoulders and shivered, my swimsuit the only thing protecting me from the Alaskan winds.

"Oh, come on," Jack urged. "It's just like jumping off a cliff... with the added benefit of holding onto something."

I shot him a look but wrapped my hands around the rope, bracing myself. "If I fall flat, you have to promise not to laugh."

"Cross my heart," he said, though the smirk on his face suggested he'd be laughing either way.

With a deep breath, I jumped, the buoy swing swinging out over the water. For a split second, I felt weightless, soaring above the sparkling surface below. Then, with a whoop, I let go, splashing down into the bay. The water was colder than I'd anticipated, shocking the air out of my lungs, but it was invigorating.

When I surfaced, Jack was still up on the rocks, laughing, his face bright with amusement. "You're a natural!"

"Your turn!" I called, challenging him. "Unless you're all talk."

"Oh, now you're asking for it." He wasted no time grabbing the rope, and with a powerful leap, he swung out over the water, releasing with a shout and landing with a bigger splash than I had. The waves washed over me, making me laugh as I splashed water back at him.

We took turns on the swing, laughing and daring each other to jump from higher and higher points on the rocks.

The buoy rope creaked and groaned, and the sun dipped lower, casting long shadows over the water. Eventually, we both lay back on the rocks, soaking in the warmth of the remaining daylight and letting the sounds of the bay settle around us.

Jack turned to me, brushing a few stray strands of seaweed from my shoulder. "Thanks for coming out here with me."

"Thanks for showing me your favorite spot," I said, smiling back at him.

He shrugged, looking almost shy. "It's better with you here."

7

As the sun dipped lower in the sky, casting warm golden light over Funter Bay, I stretched out on the soft grass, feeling a pleasant fatigue wash over me from our day of adventure. The sound of the waves lapping against the shore and the distant calls of seagulls lulled me into a peaceful state.

"I could nap here forever," I murmured, glancing over at Cassie, who was already closing her eyes. Her serene expression made me smile. I leaned back on my elbows, soaking in the beauty around us. This place felt like a slice of paradise, and I was grateful to be sharing it with Jack.

With the girls drifting off to sleep, Jack and I exchanged a look. There was a spark of mischief in his blue eyes that I couldn't resist.

"Want to go explore that little island over there?" he suggested, nodding toward a tiny, lush spot in the distance that I'd seen earlier. "I call it Cinnamon Island."

"Cinnamon Island?" I echoed, my curiosity piqued. "Why cinnamon?"

He grinned, and I felt my heart flutter. "Because there's a little spot where if you're there at just the right time, it smells distinctly of cinnamon."

I couldn't help but laugh. "Alright, lead the way, Captain Jack!"

We grabbed the kayaks we had secured to the beach earlier. I hopped into my bright yellow kayak, Jack sliding into the sleek blue one beside me. The moment we pushed off from the shore, the cool water splashed against the sides of our boats, and I felt a thrill of excitement.

Paddling in rhythm, we navigated the gentle waves, the island growing larger in the distance. Jack's laughter echoed through the air as he splashed water toward me, and I retaliated with a playful flick of my paddle. The vibrant colors of the world around us made my heart soar. The lush greenery of the trees and the deep blue of the sky seemed to blend together in a perfect symphony of nature.

After a short but exhilarating paddle, we reached the sandy shore of Cinnamon Island. I hopped out first, my feet sinking into the soft sand. "This place is amazing!" I exclaimed, taking in the untouched beauty around us. Jack joined me, securing the kayaks to a nearby tree.

"Let's find the perfect picnic spot," he said, his eyes scanning the area. I followed him as he led the way through a narrow path, pushing aside low-hanging branches. Soon, we stumbled upon a small clearing dotted with wildflowers and soft grass. It was just the right spot for our lunch.

Jack began unpacking the picnic basket he'd prepared. "I brought sandwiches, fruit, and those cookies you love," he said with a wink.

"You know me too well!" I grinned, sitting down on the grass. The smell of the salty air mixed with the sweet aroma of cookies made my stomach growl.

We sat cross-legged on the blanket, enjoying our lunch and chatting about everything and nothing. With every laugh, every shared story, I felt a deeper connection to him. The easy comfort of being together made the world outside feel like it didn't exist.

After we finished eating, I leaned back, resting my head on my arms. "This is perfect," I sighed, gazing up at the blue sky. "I could stay here forever."

Jack lay back beside me, propping his hands behind his head. "Me too. Just us, the island, and the beautiful Alaskan wilderness. What more could you want?"

His relaxed demeanor, coupled with the serene beauty of our surroundings, made my heart flutter once again. I turned to him, my curiosity getting the better of me. "So, what's the story behind Cinnamon Island?"

He chuckled, his blue eyes glinting in the sunlight. "Well, it all started when I was out here by myself one day, and I just had this moment where I felt at peace. I've come here ever since."

"That's beautiful, Jack," I said, touched by his words. "I love how you see the world."

He turned his head toward me, and for a moment, it felt like the rest of the world faded away. "And I love sharing it with you," he replied softly.

We lay there for a while, letting the warmth of the sun and the gentle sound of the waves wash over us, feeling completely at ease. With Jack by my side, I knew this was just the beginning of many more adventures to come.

* * *

The next morning, after making our way back to Juneau, we all gathered on the dock, excited for a day of exploring. The air was crisp, the kind that wakes you up with each breath, and the sun was barely peeking over the mountains. Jack waited for us with a grin, seeming as energized as the rest of us, and he led the way toward the trailhead for Nugget Falls.

We set off down the path, surrounded by towering trees and the occasional patches of sunlight breaking through the canopy. Jack kept up a steady pace, glancing back every so often to make sure we were all keeping up. I ended up walking beside him, close enough that our arms brushed every now and then, which sent little jolts of electricity through me each time.

"So, Mackerel," he said, lowering his voice as the others walked a few steps ahead. "You ready to see Alaska up close?"

I laughed, keeping my eyes on the path. "As ready as I'll ever be. Think I'll get any good material for my article out here?"

"Definitely. Though the pictures probably won't do it justice."

We followed the sound of rushing water, and soon the Nugget Falls waterfall came into view. Cascading from high above, the water thundered down in a steady rush, churning into a wide pool at its base. The sheer size of the falls took my breath away, and I saw the girls ahead pause, just as mesmerized.

"This is amazing," Sarah said, snapping photos on her phone as we neared the falls.

Cassie let out a laugh, her cheeks flushed. "I don't think I've ever seen anything this beautiful."

Jack stepped beside me, and I felt his hand brush lightly against mine, barely enough for anyone to notice. His gaze was fixed on the waterfall, a look of calm contentment on his face. "Told you Alaska had its charms," he said with a grin.

The girls started climbing over the large rocks scattered along the shoreline to get a closer look. I followed slowly, taking in every sight, every sound. The cool mist from the falls coated my face, and I closed my eyes, savoring the refreshing spray.

"This trip was exactly what I needed," I admitted, more to myself than to Jack, but he heard me.

He glanced at me with that easy smile. "Yeah? Glad to be a part of it, then."

We took turns snapping pictures, laughing as we posed in front of the falls and made silly faces. Jack stayed nearby, guiding us to the best spots for photos and helping us scramble over the slippery rocks. Every so often, he'd glance at me, a look passing between us that only we understood.

After a while, we settled on a nearby boulder to rest, watching as the morning sun began to turn the waterfall's mist into a delicate, glimmering spray.

"So, Mack," he murmured as the others chatted nearby, "think you'll be able to leave all this behind when the trip's over?"

I looked back at him, feeling the tug of Alaska—of everything I'd seen, and of this connection that had formed between us. I didn't have an answer. I didn't know if I could just walk away from this place, or from him, without it leaving some kind of mark.

"Guess we'll have to see," I said softly, giving him a small, uncertain smile.

Jack's expression softened, and in that moment, with the sound of the waterfall filling the air around us, I could almost imagine what it would be like to stay.

* * *

After our hike to Nugget Falls, everyone was ready to refuel. We drove back toward town and parked, taking our time to soak in the sights as we strolled through Juneau. When we reached a corner with a cluster of food options, Sarah and Cassie decided to grab lunch at a sandwich spot nearby, and

I glanced over to Jack, who tilted his head, a mischievous grin on his face.

"Want to try something local?" he asked, raising an eyebrow.

"Definitely," I replied, feeling that flutter in my stomach again as he led me down a quieter side street, away from the main tourist stops. We turned a corner and arrived at a small, unassuming shop with a simple sign reading Pel'meni. Inside, the warm scent of spices and buttery dough greeted us, comforting and savory.

"Pelmeni?" I asked, intrigued as we stepped up to the counter.

"They're like Russian dumplings," Jack explained, eyes twinkling with amusement. "Best comfort food around here, especially on a chilly day. You'll love them."

After ordering, we found a cozy corner to sit by the window. The restaurant was small, with a few tables scattered around, but it felt homey in a way that made me instantly relax. When our food arrived, the pelmeni were steaming hot, covered in a sprinkle of curry, fresh cilantro, and a side of sour cream and rye bread. I took a bite and melted a little at the rich, savory flavor.

"Oh my god," I said, almost forgetting myself as I looked up at him, my eyes wide. "This is amazing."

Jack laughed, leaning back as he took a bite of his own. "I had a feeling you'd like it."

The conversation flowed easily as we ate, dipping dumplings in sour cream and talking about everything from travel to work. I told him a little about the article I was working on, and he shared some of the highs and lows of life working on a boat in Alaska. I felt myself relaxing, leaning into the moment, and letting my guard down as I listened to him talk.

"Is this what you always wanted to do?" I asked, genuinely curious as he finished his last bite.

Jack shrugged, gazing out the window thoughtfully. "Not always. I've done a lot of different things—bartending was just supposed to be temporary, but then I got here, started working on the boats, and I just... liked it. Being out on the water, seeing Alaska every day. I don't think I'll ever get tired of it."

I nodded, understanding that pull more than I expected. There was something magical about Alaska, this raw beauty that seemed to touch everyone who experienced it. As I looked at Jack, I felt myself slipping a little more, wanting to know every part of him.

"So, what about you?" he asked, leaning forward with a grin. "Do you love writing as much as you thought you would?"

I hesitated, then nodded. "Most days, yeah. But sometimes... I don't know. I think about whether I want to do something else, something that lets me be a little more... present."

Jack's expression softened. "I get that. But if it brought you here, it's gotta be worth something, right?"

I felt myself blush, looking down at my empty plate to hide it. "Yeah, maybe you're right."

When we finished, we lingered a little longer, both of us reluctant to leave the cozy little restaurant. Eventually, Jack glanced at his watch and sighed.

"Ready to get back to the others?" he asked, though he didn't look eager to go, either.

I nodded, but I knew this day had shifted something between us, that it wouldn't be easy to brush aside the way he made me feel. As we walked back toward the main street, he brushed his hand against mine, just lightly, almost testing the waters. I looked up at him, and he gave me a shy, almost hesitant smile, like he was hoping I felt the same spark.

And, of course, I did.

* * *

After lunch, Jack and I wandered back through down-town Juneau, our steps unhurried as we explored the local shops lining the streets. We ducked into a few places, browsing through hand-carved totems, local art prints, and cozy flannel shirts, laughing as we held up ridiculous hats for each other to try. The afternoon was slipping by, each moment feeling a little dreamier than the last.

Just as we passed a store with a large, enticing window display, Jack stopped and gave me a knowing grin. "Ever been to the Alaskan Fudge Company?"

"No, but with a name like that, how can I say no?" I replied, my sweet tooth perking up immediately.

He held the door open for me, and we were met with the most heavenly scent of warm chocolate, caramel, and butter. Inside, shelves and display cases were filled with everything from chocolate-covered caramels to almond bark, chocolate-dipped Oreos, and truffles. There was even a glass counter where they were making fresh fudge, thick swirls of chocolate poured and spread out with wide metal paddles.

"Okay, this is already my favorite place in Alaska," I said, transfixed by the array of sweets in front of me.

Jack chuckled, nudging me toward the counter. "You haven't even tried it yet. Go ahead, pick something."

I scanned the display, my eyes landing on a tray labeled "Glacier Fudge" — a smooth, creamy white chocolate fudge swirled with blue. "What's that one?" I asked the woman behind the counter.

"That's our specialty — white chocolate and blueberry," she explained with a smile. "And don't worry, we offer free samples."

She handed me a small square, and I took a bite, closing my eyes as the creamy sweetness melted on my tongue with the subtle tang of blueberries. "Oh my god, this is amazing," I said, savoring it.

Jack grabbed a sample of a dark chocolate walnut fudge, taking a bite as he looked at me, an amused glint in his eye. "Pretty good, right?"

"Good doesn't even cover it," I replied, already reaching for my wallet to buy a small box. Jack followed suit, and soon we were outside, each of us carrying a bag filled with a few selections of fudge to take back to the boat.

As we walked down the street, I popped another bite of Glacier Fudge in my mouth, unable to resist. "I think I'm going to be ruined for regular chocolate after this."

Jack laughed, taking a piece from his own stash. "I don't think I could go a week without the stuff now. It's one of my favorite stops here."

"Well, now it's officially one of mine, too," I said, flashing him a grin.

We walked along, pausing every now and then to take in the shops and the passing boats in the harbor. When we reached a quiet stretch of sidewalk, Jack offered me his arm, half-jokingly, half-sincere, and I accepted, laughing as he led us back toward the water.

* * *

That evening, back on the boat, I settled into a cozy corner of the lounge with my laptop, ready to dive into my writing. I hadn't touched my draft in a few days, letting the experience of Alaska soak in without a filter. But now, with so many moments swimming around in my head, I couldn't wait to capture them. Each memory felt like a postcard I wanted to pin down before it slipped away.

I started typing, recounting the incredible scenes that had already filled my trip: our first day cruising through Tracy Arm Fjord, watching sea lions nap on blue icebergs, and paddling in kayaks past towering glaciers. I could practically feel the icy mist on my face again as I typed, describing the peaceful stillness, the vast, humbling beauty.

And then there was Hoonah — the thrill of the zipline, that exhilarating second when I let go of all my fears and just soared above the green treetops. I remembered the ache of my sides from laughing with the girls afterward, still high from the adrenaline and practically giddy from the adventure. The smell of fresh crab, the way it melted in my mouth after our crab pot haul, the freshness of the sea somehow baked right into the flavor.

As I relived the moments on the page, though, I couldn't help but realize how much Jack had already woven himself into these memories. He'd been there for almost every highlight, from showing us his favorite places to teasing me about trying on his clunky Xtratuf boots to finally learning how to fish off the side of the boat. He was in all the little details, the laughter, the warmth that had made this trip feel like more than just a series of destinations.

I paused, fingers hovering over the keyboard as I thought about how he'd handed me that bite of Glacier Fudge earlier today, the smile in his eyes as if he already knew I'd fall for it. It was those little moments that were somehow making the trip feel special in a way I hadn't expected. Was it... was he... was I falling for him?

I glanced down at my notes, my heart doing a small, unexpected flutter at the thought. Including him in my story felt like the most natural thing in the world. It was as though he'd become part of this experience, a thread I couldn't untangle even if I tried.

I paused, wondering if I should include all these details. Was it strange to write about him? Maybe it was, but pretending he hadn't been a part of this trip felt dishonest, like I'd be leaving out something vital. Jack had become more than just a passing character in my adventure here. Alaska wasn't simply a series of mountains and seas and towns; it had been a place where I'd felt something new start to take root.

The cursor blinked, waiting for my next move, and I found myself smiling, imagining Jack's reaction to reading this someday. My fingers flew over the keys as I poured out stories from the past days, letting him become part of the adventure in every way he already had.

8

The next morning, we set out early, excitement buzzing through us as we made our way to the tram station in downtown Juneau. The tram cars, bright red against the green and gray of the mountains, looked almost like they belonged in a fairytale.

Jack handed me my ticket with a little smile. "Ready to go sky-high, Mack?"

"Only if you promise not to freak out," I teased, nudging him in the arm.

He chuckled, shaking his head. "Oh, you're on, Mack."

The tram car doors opened, and we stepped inside with the rest of the group, everyone pressing close to the windows. As soon as we started to rise, the entire town of Juneau sprawled out below, the rooftops getting smaller and the boats in the harbor shrinking to toy size. I felt my stomach do a little flip — from the height or the view, I wasn't sure.

The tram rose higher and higher, gliding smoothly up the steep mountainside. The dense forest on either side of us stretched endlessly, with evergreens that looked like a lush green blanket hugging the rocky cliffs. The higher we climbed, the quieter the cabin became, everyone's eyes glued to the panorama unfolding outside. The air felt cooler as we ascended, a faint, earthy scent seeping through the tram's windows.

I glanced over at Jack, and he was staring out the window too, his expression softened, as if seeing something that spoke to him. He caught me looking and grinned, a bit sheepishly. "I don't think I'll ever get used to this," he said, nodding toward the view.

"You're telling me," I whispered. "It's like stepping into another world."

When the tram finally reached the top, we filed out onto the viewing platform. The Mount Roberts Visitor Center was perched at the edge of the cliff, surrounded by trails that wove up through the misty mountaintop. We wandered along the platform, taking in the view that stretched out endlessly in all directions — mountains rolling into the distance, layered in hues of green and blue, with slivers of ocean glinting through.

"It feels unreal," I murmured, leaning on the railing next to Jack. He was standing so close that our shoulders touched, and for a moment, it felt like the rest of the world faded away, leaving just us and this spectacular view.

"Glad you're here to see it," Jack said softly. I looked up at him, catching a look in his eyes that was tender, almost vulnerable. Before I could think too hard about it, he straightened, a teasing glint in his eyes. "And to think you were going to try and bail on me yesterday," he added, nudging me with his elbow.

I laughed, rolling my eyes. "As if you'd let me."

We wandered the trails a bit longer, stopping to watch a few mountain goats picking their way along the cliffside. The air was fresh, and the scenery around us was wild and untouched, with wildflowers peeking up through the rocky soil. It felt like we'd been given a special view into a part of Alaska most people never saw, and I couldn't have imagined a better way to experience it.

After soaking up every bit of the mountain views, we wandered into the cozy little gift shop inside the visitor center. The shop was filled with all kinds of Alaskan treasures: carved totems, tiny bottles of wild blueberry jam, polished stones, and racks of soft, hand-knit scarves. I ran my fingers along a display of hand-carved figurines, admiring the intricate details and wondering about the stories behind each one.

"This place has charm," Jack said, picking up a small ivory bear carved with tiny, lifelike details.

"More charm than your average gift shop, that's for sure," I replied, thumbing through postcards with moose and salmon splashed across them.

As we browsed, a small, hand-painted sign near the back caught my eye: Presentation on Native Alaskan Tribes Starting Soon in Theater. I nudged Jack. "Want to go learn something?"

He grinned, slipping the bear figurine back on the shelf. "Sounds like a plan."

We found seats in the back row of a small theater, dimly lit and cozy, with walls decorated in traditional patterns and motifs. A few more visitors settled into seats around us as the lights dimmed further, and the screen at the front flickered to life.

The video opened with sweeping shots of glaciers and rivers, then shifted to quiet, respectful portraits of members of the Tlingit, Haida, and Tsimshian tribes, the narrators speaking in soft, reverent tones about the people who had lived and thrived on this land for thousands of years. The film moved through their traditions — woodcarving, totem making, and fishing, as well as celebrations of family and the land that provided for them. Watching the video, I felt like I was catching glimpses of a life deeply connected to nature, one that held an unbroken line back through history.

The narrator's voice rose as the scene shifted to a shot of the Tlingit totem poles, tall and proud against the backdrop of evergreen trees. Each symbol, we learned, held stories passed down through generations — legends of animals, ancestors, and nature woven together to explain their world and honor their heritage.

I glanced over at Jack, his expression serious, thoughtful. He must have sensed me looking because he turned and gave me a small, soft smile, his eyes reflecting some of the same awe I was feeling.

When the lights came back up, we sat for a moment, not quite ready to leave. "That was incredible," I whispered.

"It really was," Jack agreed. "To think of all the stories these mountains and rivers must hold." He glanced toward the door, then back at me, his smile tinged with something contemplative. "Kind of puts things into perspective, doesn't it?"

I nodded, a warmth blooming inside me. We left the theater quietly, and as we stepped back out into the bustling visitor center, I felt a renewed sense of respect for the land around us — and an even stronger connection to Jack, knowing we'd shared something that felt so profound.

After the video, we walked toward the doors that led outside, and we came across a large mural painted on one of the walls. It depicted all the bears native to Alaska, standing up on their hind legs with measurements next to them. They were towering above us — even the black bear, which was labeled as the smallest of the three types. But the brown and polar bears were a different story entirely. At over ten feet, the polar bear seemed impossibly huge.

Jack stood up close to the mural, stretching his hand as high as he could over his head to try and reach the top of the black bear's size. "Alright, Mack," he said, turning back with a grin, "think I'm a match?"

"Hmm, maybe you could take on the black bear," I said, laughing. "But I think the brown and polar bears have you beat."

He placed his hand over his heart, feigning offense. "You doubt my bear-fighting abilities?"

"Absolutely," I replied, trying to hold back a smile. "Although maybe you're tall enough to spook a bear cub."

"Very funny," he said, sidling up next to me and pretending to tower over me with his best "bear growl," which was more goofy than intimidating.

I couldn't help but laugh, shaking my head at him. "Alright, alright, I'll admit it — you're kind of intimidating."

Jack gave me a triumphant grin, but then we both looked up at the polar bear's height again. The size of it put us right back into that shared sense of awe we'd felt in the theater.

"Can you imagine running into something that big out here?" I asked, genuinely impressed.

Jack whistled softly. "I'll stick with eagles' nests and fish, thanks. Those bears are amazing, but maybe best seen from a good, safe distance."

"Agreed," I said, smiling as we took one last look at the mural before heading out toward the trail. Being up here felt both peaceful and wild, and I couldn't help but feel grateful for every new piece of this adventure. And sharing it with Jack, even our little jokes, just made it all the more special.

We stepped outside and were greeted by a fresh mountain breeze. The trails around the visitor center wound through clusters of evergreens, dotted with information signs about local wildlife. I could hear Jack's footsteps crunching beside me as we wandered along, taking in the crisp air and the quiet.

A few steps down the path, we spotted a massive eagle's nest perched high up in a towering tree. It was layered and knotted with branches and leaves, looking like it had been there for years — maybe even decades.

"Wow, look at that!" I said, pointing. "I knew bald eagles' nests were big, but that's like... treehouse big."

Jack laughed, tilting his head up to take it all in. "Wouldn't want to be under that if it ever came down," he joked. "Imagine how much work it takes for them to build it, though."

I imagined a pair of eagles hauling branches up one by one, twisting and securing them in place with precision. "It's kind of amazing, isn't it? Like they're building their own little mountain fort up there."

After a few minutes of wandering around, we decided to head back to the visitor's center to catch up with Sarah and Cassie.

"Hey there," Cassie said with a small grin, "we've been looking for you, what have you been up to?"

"Nothing," I replied innocently.

But the flirting and banter Jack and I shared certainly didn't feel like nothing.

* * *

As we made our way back down the tram and returned to the harbor, Jack suggested we stop by the whale sculpture just down the path.

"You'll love this," he said, nudging my shoulder. "It's like seeing one of those whales up close again, without the sea spray."

A few minutes later, we arrived at the "Whale Project" — a massive bronze sculpture of a humpback whale mid-breach, frozen in a graceful arch as though it had leapt right out of the water. Water sprayed from jets around it, creating an illusion of the ocean and a scene of stunning, permanent movement.

"Wow," I whispered, circling it slowly. "It's like the real thing. Look at the details on its fins and tail."

The whale's body was larger than life, with every line of its skin etched deeply, capturing the rough texture and majesty of an actual humpback. The fountain around it added to the illusion, misting the air lightly. I could almost imagine it alive, just like the ones we'd watched days ago.

"Think it looks like the one we saw breaching out by Hoonah?" Jack asked, coming up beside me. He was staring up at the whale's towering form with the same awe I felt.

I nodded, my mind flashing back to that day. "It does. Although this one is a bit friendlier than seeing one that close in open water."

He chuckled. "Yeah, less chance of a rogue tail splash. But just imagine... I mean, they're really that big."

We stepped back to take in the full view, and I could feel my heart race a little. Seeing the sculpture here, right on the edge of the harbor, was so different from seeing whales out in the open ocean. There, they were untouchable, mysterious. Here, they felt almost within reach, like a bridge between worlds.

"Look," Jack said, gesturing to a plaque beside the sculpture. It detailed the artist's vision and the importance of the whale in Alaskan waters, its role as both an icon and a symbol of conservation efforts.

"Do you think anyone can really capture how big they are?" I asked, thinking about how enormous they had looked gliding through the water, dwarfing our boat as we watched, spellbound. "Like, even seeing this, it still feels impossible that they're real."

Jack looked down at me, a smile tugging at his lips. "Guess that's part of why we keep coming back, isn't it? To try to understand what we can't really explain."

I thought about that for a moment. Jack was right; seeing something like this, something beyond the everyday, was exactly why I'd come to Alaska. For the adventure, the mystery, the things that made you feel both incredibly small and incredibly alive.

As we walked around the sculpture one last time, I couldn't shake the feeling that this trip, these experiences — even meeting Jack — were becoming a part of something much bigger than I had planned.

* * *

After we finished admiring the whale sculpture, we made our way back to the boat in comfortable silence. The gentle swaying as we boarded felt more familiar now, like coming home. The other girls were already back in their cabins, and after exchanging goodnights with Jack, I headed into my own. I changed into my pajamas, brushed my teeth, and settled in, but sleep felt miles away. I stared up at the low ceiling, my mind spinning with the day's events and memories of each moment spent with Jack. Every time I closed my eyes, I saw him smiling, laughing, or quietly watching me from across the table.

I glanced at the clock on my phone. Midnight. I sighed and turned over, but it was no use. My dream from nights ago crept back into my mind — the one where I'd found Jack on the bow under the stars, the ocean stretching out around us. Maybe some fresh air would help. Without thinking much more about it, I threw on a light jacket and stepped outside.

The deck was almost pitch-black, save for the faint light of the moon casting a shimmering trail across the water. My footsteps felt amplified in the quiet, but as I rounded the corner to the bow, I saw a shadowy figure leaning against the railing, gazing out at the open water. My heart skipped. It was Jack.

His head turned as I approached, and he smiled softly. "Couldn't sleep?"

I shook my head, feeling a little bashful. "Guess the day was too exciting. You, too?"

He nodded, then gestured to the spot next to him. I joined him at the rail, and we stood in silence for a moment, the sound of the water sloshing gently against the boat. The air was cool, with just a hint of salt, and the whole scene felt like something out of my dream.

"It's strange," he said softly, his voice barely louder than the waves. "I spend so many nights out here like this, just listening to the ocean. But tonight feels...different."

I glanced over at him, feeling my cheeks heat up. "Yeah? How so?"

He looked at me, eyes soft and reflective. "I think it's the company." His smile grew a bit as he looked back out over the water. "I've really liked getting to know you, Mackenzie."

"Same," I replied, surprised by the steadiness in my voice. "This trip...it's been everything I wanted and more. And I didn't expect...well, you." I shrugged, not quite knowing how to put it into words.

He chuckled softly. "I guess I didn't expect you, either."

We were quiet for a while, just listening to the night. The tension between us seemed to hang in the air, a question waiting to be answered.

"Do you believe in things happening for a reason?" he asked, his voice barely a whisper.

I turned to look at him, our faces close in the dim light. "I think so. Do you?"

His eyes lingered on mine. "Yeah. Especially now."

And before I could say anything, he leaned in, closing the distance between us. His lips brushed mine, gentle at first, as if giving me a chance to pull away. But I didn't want to. I leaned into him, feeling the warmth of his hand as it rested softly on my back, grounding me to this moment that felt like it had been a long time coming.

When we finally pulled apart, I felt like I was floating, my heart racing. He smiled, looking a bit shy himself for once. "Guess we both needed that," he murmured.

"Guess so," I replied, a small laugh slipping out. We stood there a while longer, watching the moonlight dance on the waves, neither of us wanting to be the first to go back inside. Tonight, this moment was ours, out on the bow, where the world felt like it had shrunk down to just the two of us.

9

The next morning, I slipped into the dining area of the boat where the girls were already huddled around a table, forks in hand, chatting over steaming cups of coffee. I grabbed a plate, heaping it with scrambled eggs, toast, and fresh fruit, and slid into the last seat beside them.

"Morning, Mackenzie," Sarah said with a grin. She glanced at me, eyebrows raised. "You look...extra chipper today."

I tried to play it cool, but I could feel the warmth rising to my cheeks. "Morning," I mumbled, taking a long sip of coffee.

Sarah shot a glance to Cassie, who smirked knowingly. "Okay, spill it," Cassie said, folding her arms. "What's up with you?"

I laughed, shaking my head. "What do you mean?"

"Oh, please." Sarah leaned in, narrowing her eyes playfully. "I know that look. You've been holding something back since you walked in here. Out with it!"

I looked down at my coffee, biting back a smile. The memory of last night's kiss was still so fresh, as if it had just happened. Finally, I took a deep breath. "Alright, fine. I...kissed Jack last night."

The girls gasped in unison, and Sarah nearly dropped her fork. "Wait, what? Our Jack?"

"Yes, *our* Jack," I replied, laughing at her dramatic reaction.

Cassie slapped the table, grinning. "No way! Tell us everything!"

I couldn't help but smile as I recounted last night — how I'd found him on the bow under the stars, the way he'd looked at me, and how natural it had felt to finally kiss him. By the time I finished, the girls were grinning ear to ear.

"Oh my gosh," Sarah sighed dreamily. "That sounds like something straight out of a romance novel."

"It kind of felt like one, honestly," I admitted, laughing. "I mean, the ocean, the moonlight...it was surreal."

Sarah leaned forward, her face all excitement. "So, what happens now?"

I paused, the question tugging at the back of my mind. "I'm not sure," I admitted. "I mean, we've only known each other for, what, a week? And I'm going back home after this trip, so...I don't know. I guess I'm just enjoying the moment."

Cassie tilted her head, studying me. "But it sounds like there's more there than just a little vacation fling."

"Maybe," I said, my voice softening. "It's just...there's something about him. I can't explain it."

Sarah sighed, her eyes dreamy. "I say enjoy it. You never know where things like this might lead, right?"

I nodded, my mind drifting back to the feel of Jack's hand on my back, the way he'd looked at me under the stars. "Yeah, maybe you're right. I think I will."

The girls exchanged glances, smiling as if they already knew the answer to questions I hadn't even fully formed yet. And as we finished breakfast, I couldn't help but wonder just what this trip might mean for me — not just as a vacation, but as something that could change my life in ways I hadn't expected.

* * *

As the girls split off to explore the local shops and indulge in some souvenirs, Jack and I set off toward the trail that would lead us up to the glacier. The morning air was crisp, tinged with the scent of pine and a hint of cold glacier runoff. Jack led the way, his steps sure and easy, while I followed, feeling a blend of excitement and nervous energy bubbling up inside me.

"I hope you're up for a bit of a workout," he said, flashing me a grin over his shoulder. "This trail's got a few steep sections."

"I'll try to keep up," I replied, laughing as I adjusted the straps on my backpack. "But if I fall behind, just promise you won't leave me for the bears."

He chuckled. "Not a chance. I'd miss the company too much."

We trekked up through dense forest that opened every so often to breathtaking views of the valley below. The trail wound and climbed, and as we moved higher, the distant blue shimmer of the glacier came into view. Jack pointed it out, his voice taking on a reverent tone.

"There she is. That's Mendenhall Glacier. It's incredible, right?"

I nodded, unable to find the right words. "Incredible doesn't even cover it."

The glacier was massive and surreal, like something from another world. Its ice was a brilliant shade of blue, reflecting light like a jewel tucked into the mountains. As we walked closer, the remnants of old mining equipment scattered along the trail began to appear — rusty gears and sections of track, partially buried in the earth and overgrown with moss and lichen.

"Is this from the mining days?" I asked, stepping over a piece of what looked like an old rail.

"Yeah," Jack nodded, brushing his hand over one of the machines. "A lot of this equipment was abandoned after the gold rush ended. People left in a hurry, taking only what they could carry and leaving everything else behind."

I crouched down to inspect the intricate metal gears, half-buried in the earth. "It's like stepping back in time."

Jack stood beside me, hands in his pockets as he looked out toward the glacier. "There's something kind of humbling about it. Nature just takes back what's hers, no matter what we build or leave behind."

For a moment, we both fell silent, caught up in the raw beauty of it all. Finally, he offered me his hand, helping me up as we made our way to a nearby rock that offered a clear view of the glacier. We sat there, side by side, in comfortable silence, just watching the icy landscape.

After a few minutes, he spoke up, his voice softer. "I've brought people up here before, but...it feels different today."

My heart skipped a beat. "Different, how?"

He looked at me, the warmth in his eyes matching his soft smile. "Well, this time, I actually wanted to be here."

My cheeks flushed, but I tried to keep my voice steady. "I'm glad you're here too. Really."

We sat for a while longer, just talking about everything and nothing, sharing stories and laughs as if we'd known each other for much longer than a week. Finally, with the sun inching closer to the horizon, we made our way back down the trail, the moment lingering like an unspoken promise between us.

As we started down the trail, Jack slowed suddenly and raised a hand, gesturing for me to stop. My heart stilled as I followed his gaze to a patch of brush just off the trail. There, only about twenty yards away, was a massive brown bear with two small cubs beside her, tumbling over each other as they played.

"Oh my gosh," I whispered, eyes wide. "Jack, look!"

He gave a subtle nod, a small grin playing on his lips. "Pretty amazing, right? But keep your voice low — and no sudden moves. We don't want her feeling like we're too close."

I was already frozen in place, mesmerized by the bears. The mother bear was stunning, her thick brown coat catching the afternoon light. She gave her cubs a gentle nudge, and they rolled playfully, oblivious to everything else. The sight was surreal, and my heart pounded in a mix of excitement and awe.

"I can't believe this," I whispered, barely able to contain my giddiness. "I never thought I'd see bears this close. Look at those little faces!"

The cubs clambered over each other, one nipping the other's ear, then pausing to look around before waddling to their mother's side. The mother bear watched us with calm awareness, then returned her attention to her playful cubs, as though deciding we weren't a threat.

Jack leaned toward me slightly. "It's incredible, isn't it?" he murmured. "They're so wild and...powerful."

"It's like watching a scene from a nature documentary," I replied, barely able to tear my eyes away. "I can't believe how calm she is. It's like...she trusts us."

"Or she just knows she's stronger than anything out here," Jack said, his voice a soft laugh.

We watched in silence for a few more moments, completely captivated by the small family of bears. Eventually, the mother bear let out a low huff and nudged her cubs, steering them back into the trees. The cubs trailed after her reluctantly, glancing back as they vanished into the brush.

I let out a breath I didn't realize I'd been holding. "I think that was one of the best moments of my life," I said, feeling a deep thrill in my chest. "Thank you for bringing me here, Jack."

He gave me a warm, lingering look. "It was my pleasure, Mackenzie. That look on your face? Totally worth it."

With hearts still pounding from the encounter, we continued down the trail, the magic of the moment lingering between us like a quiet, shared secret.

* * *

Back in my cabin, I settled onto my bed, laptop balanced on my knees. I opened a fresh document, ready to capture everything that had happened that day — every thrill, every moment of awe. I started typing, recounting the hike, the glistening glacier, and finally, the heart-stopping moment when we'd spotted the bear and her cubs. Just writing about it brought back the giddiness I'd felt, the hushed silence of the forest, and the warmth of Jack standing beside me. The memory still filled me with a bubbling excitement that was hard to shake.

As I wrote, I found myself lingering over the moments with Jack, especially when he'd looked at me with that warm, knowing smile. Something had shifted between us in those quiet moments. It wasn't just about Alaska anymore — it was about him, too.

I paused, fingers hovering above the keyboard. Did I dare include him in the story? This book was supposed to be about the wonders of Alaska, not about the bartender who had somehow slipped under my skin. And yet, he'd become such a part of this experience, as much a part of it as the mountains, the glaciers, and the endless ocean.

With a smile, I started typing again, weaving in details about him — the way he laughed, how he shared his knowledge about the land, the easy confidence he had that was, somehow, starting to feel safe.

After finishing up the last paragraph, I finally closed my laptop, a contented sigh slipping out as I stretched. The day had been unforgettable, and now, recording it felt like preserving a piece of this amazing trip.

As I got ready for bed, the excitement of everything settled into a warm, happy buzz. I brushed my teeth, climbed into bed, and let my head sink into the pillow. But sleep didn't come easily. I found myself wide awake, mind replaying every moment with Jack, the soft thrill of his gaze, the way he'd called me "Mack."

The night was quiet, the gentle sway of the boat lulling me into a calm I couldn't quite surrender to. I drifted to the edge of sleep, only to be pulled back again by thoughts of him. With a sigh, I flipped onto my side, gazing out the small window, where the dark sea stretched toward the horizon under a blanket of stars.

Eventually, I gave in to my restless thoughts, curling deeper under the covers with a soft smile and letting myself fall asleep with Jack on my mind.

* * *

The next morning, I sat on the edge of my bed, phone pressed to my ear, waiting for my editor to pick up. The familiar New York City buzz sounded faintly through the speaker as his voice finally came on.

"Mackenzie! How's Alaska?" he greeted, sounding as if he were already rushing between meetings.

"It's... incredible," I replied, a smile slipping onto my face. "But I wanted to ask you something... a little more serious."

There was a pause, and then, "Sure, shoot."

I took a breath. "Do you think it would be possible for me to work remotely... long-term? Like, from somewhere outside New York?"

He was quiet for a moment before responding, his tone hesitant. "You know I love your work, Mackenzie. And if anyone could pull it off, it'd be you. But... New York is the heart of things. The connections, the events, the pulse — that's what keeps your career moving forward."

"So, you don't think it's realistic?" I asked, my voice softer, already knowing his answer.

"It's not that I don't think you could try," he replied, choosing his words carefully. "But it would mean fewer opportunities, fewer face-to-face meetings, and possibly, fewer big projects down the line. Not that I doubt your talent — it's just... harder from afar."

I nodded, even though he couldn't see me. "Got it," I said, swallowing the pang of disappointment.

"Take it in stride, Mackenzie," he continued, more gently. "Enjoy Alaska, get all the inspiration you can, and let's keep you as one of our top writers. We'll figure out ways to work with whatever you need, but... maybe hold onto New York for a while longer?"

"Yeah," I said, trying to sound lighter than I felt. "Thanks for being honest."

"Anytime. And hey, can't wait to see what you've been writing while you're out there! Catch you soon?"

"Of course," I replied, forcing a smile as we said our good-byes.

When I finally set the phone down, a quiet resolve settled over me. Could I really make this choice between my life in New York and... maybe, something more here? The answer felt like it was slipping through my fingers, hidden somewhere in the glinting waves of the Alaskan waters and the uncharted path stretching before me.

As I sat in the dim light of the boat cabin, the gentle sway of the waves rocked me, but it did little to soothe the storm brewing inside. I stared at the pages spread out on the small table, the words blurring as I tried to focus on the story I'd been working on. It was supposed to be my escape, a chance to pour my heart into a narrative that felt safe, but instead, it had become a constant reminder of everything I was trying to work through.

My editor's words echoed in my mind: "Mackenzie, moving to Alaska is a mistake. You can't let a relationship jeopardize your writing career." Each time I replayed it, the weight of her disapproval pressed down on me like the heavy, humid air before a storm. I understood the practicality behind her advice, but it felt wrong, as if I were being asked to choose between two parts of myself—my career and my heart.

I leaned back in my chair, the wood creaking softly under my weight, and closed my eyes, letting my thoughts drift to Jack. Memories of him flooded my mind: the way he laughed, the spark in his eyes when he talked about the ocean, the feeling of safety I'd found in his presence. It was so easy to imagine a life here with him, full of adventure and discovery.

Maybe my editor was right. Maybe chasing a relationship was a risk I couldn't afford to take. But how could I dismiss what I felt for Jack? Each day, I thought of him—wondering what he was doing, how his business was faring, if he was still taking people out to Cinnamon Island. I longed for those moments we'd shared, the feeling of being completely understood, of being seen.

But here I was, sitting in a boat cabin, away from my job, my life in New York, and the dreams I'd built. I picked up my pen and absently doodled on the margin of my notes. Would my writing ever feel whole again if I couldn't embrace the beauty of my time with Jack?

I glanced out the small window, watching the sunlight glimmer on the water, and the thought crept in—what if I didn't have to choose? What if I could find a way to integrate both worlds? My heart raced at the possibility, but fear gripped me. I didn't want to set myself up for disappointment again, didn't want to dive headfirst into something that could leave me shattered.

10

The next morning, excitement buzzed through the air as we made our way to the dock for our floatplane tour. The seaplane gleamed in the early morning light, bobbing gently on the harbor waters as it awaited us. The vastness of the mountains around us seemed even more magnificent now that we were about to take to the sky and see it all from above.

Jack held my hand as we walked across the dock, his enthusiasm contagious. Sarah and I exchanged excited glances, and even the usually composed Jack seemed to be holding back a grin.

We boarded the floatplane, and the pilot, a cheerful man named Tom, welcomed us with a warm smile. "You picked a perfect day for a flight," he said, nodding toward the clear blue sky. "We'll be heading over the glaciers, and if we're lucky, you might even spot some wildlife down below. Keep those cameras ready!"

We buckled in, the soft hum of the plane filling the small cabin as Tom went through his final checks. Then, with a gentle lurch, the plane began to glide over the water, picking up speed. I glanced out the window, feeling a flutter of excitement mixed with a tiny bit of nerves. Just as we reached the end of the harbor, the plane lifted off the water, and I felt the rush of weightlessness as we soared into the sky.

Below us, Juneau spread out like a miniature town in a snow globe, each building tiny and perfect. The ocean glittered in the sunlight, and the lush, forested mountains rose up around the town, giving it an almost magical quality from above.

"Look at that view!" Sarah's voice was filled with awe as she pressed her face to the window, taking in the beauty beneath us.

I couldn't look away, the vastness of the Alaskan wilderness stretching out in every direction. Snow-capped peaks rolled on endlessly, and just ahead, the glaciers came into view, their icy blue depths cutting through the mountains. Rivers of ice wound through valleys, glinting in the sunlight, and crevasses as deep as city buildings split the glaciers in jagged lines. I had never seen anything like it.

"That's the Taku Glacier," Tom said through our headsets, pointing out the window. "One of the largest in the region. It's been here for thousands of years, carving its way through these mountains."

Jack's hand squeezed mine as he pointed toward the glacier. "Can you believe something that massive could be made of ice?"

"It's incredible," I whispered, feeling humbled by the scale and power of nature.

Tom dipped the plane lower, and we had a closer view of the glacier, the deep blue cracks almost glowing against the white snow. Every turn of the plane revealed new sights—mountain peaks sharp and jagged, untouched forests, and hidden lakes nestled like secrets in the valleys below.

At one point, we spotted a herd of mountain goats, small white dots moving gracefully along a cliffside. Tom pointed them out with a chuckle. "Only in Alaska can you see wildlife like that from up here."

We circled back toward Juneau, passing over the Mendenhall Glacier and its lake, where the chunks of floating ice shimmered like scattered jewels in the water. As we flew closer to the town, I could see the familiar sights of the harbor and the colorful buildings lining the streets, each one tiny from our perspective up here.

Tom made a wide, graceful turn, preparing for our descent. My heart skipped a beat as I looked down at the harbor, realizing we'd be landing back on the water. As we approached, the pilot expertly guided the floatplane down, and with a gentle splash, we touched down on the water, gliding smoothly before coming to a slow stop.

I let out a breath I hadn't realized I was holding, a huge smile on my face as I turned to the others. Sarah was grinning ear to ear, and Jack looked exhilarated, his eyes bright as he met mine.

"That was amazing," I said, feeling a thrill of excitement still buzzing in my veins.

Jack laughed, his gaze lingering on mine. "Alaska has a way of surprising you, doesn't it?"

As we climbed out of the plane and onto the dock, I knew this was a memory I'd hold onto forever. Alaska was unlike any place I'd ever been, and sharing it with Jack and Sarah made it all the more unforgettable.

* * *

The ride back to the boat was quiet, each of us lost in our own thoughts after the breathtaking flight. Once we reached the dock, Sarah wandered off to the other side of the boat, giving us some space. Jack and I stayed on deck, watching the water ripple softly against the hull, the afternoon sun casting golden light over the harbor.

Jack leaned against the railing, his gaze fixed on the mountains in the distance. His hand was resting close to mine, but there was a tension in the air that hadn't been there before. I'd felt it growing over the past few days—a distance beneath all the laughter and shared glances. Now, with our trip winding down, it felt like everything we hadn't said was pressing in on us.

I took a deep breath, breaking the silence. "It's going to be hard to leave all of this," I said softly, my voice carrying a hint of the worry that had been tugging at me since we'd arrived in Alaska.

Jack nodded, his jaw tightening slightly. "Yeah, it is. This place... it feels like home to me, you know?"

I looked at him, really looked, and saw the way his eyes held a quiet sadness. "You've built a life here, Jack. And I love seeing you in it. You belong here."

He glanced at me, a flicker of pain in his eyes. "But you... your life is somewhere else. Your family, your job—it's all back there. You have a whole world waiting for you."

I felt my heart sink as he voiced the thoughts that had been circling in my mind. "I know," I whispered, swallowing against the lump in my throat. "I want to be with you, but... how would it work? I don't want to make you leave all of this behind. I'd never ask that of you."

Jack's gaze softened, and he reached out, taking my hand in his. "And I don't want to be the reason you give up everything you've worked for. I could never ask you to do that, Mackenzie."

We stood in silence for a moment, holding each other's hands as the gentle waves rocked the boat. The weight of our words felt crushing—each one laying out the reality we'd been avoiding.

"But I also can't imagine not being with you," he said, his voice barely above a whisper. "Every time I think about you going back, about us... ending, it feels like I'm losing a part of myself."

My heart ached at his words, the raw vulnerability in his voice. "I feel the same way," I admitted, my voice trembling. "But is love enough if we're thousands of miles apart? I don't want to just be a visitor in your life, popping in and out. And I know you deserve more than that, too."

Jack looked away, his jaw clenched as he tried to control his emotions. "It's just... damn, Mackenzie, I wish it didn't have to be so complicated. If it were just you and me, here in this moment, it would all make sense."

I nodded, squeezing his hand as we both tried to find a way around the impossible choice in front of us. "Maybe we just...

give it time?" I said, my voice shaky. "We can't know what the future holds, but maybe if we try, we'll find a way to make this work."

He looked back at me, a glimmer of hope in his eyes. "Yeah, maybe. We don't have to figure it all out today." He pulled me close, his arms wrapping around me as he rested his chin on the top of my head. "But whatever happens, I'm not giving up on us. Not until we've tried everything."

I wrapped my arms around him, holding on tight as I felt the weight of our words settle. We didn't have all the answers, and the future looked uncertain and daunting. But in this moment, with his arms around me and the Alaskan sun setting behind us, I felt a glimmer of hope.

"We'll find a way," I whispered, more to myself than to him, a quiet promise to both of us. "One way or another."

* * *

The final day of our trip arrived faster than I wanted it to. It was the Fourth of July, and the energy around Juneau was electric. Jack had taken us to the heart of the harbor downtown, and all around us, boats lined up in anticipation, their decks strung with lights and flags flapping in the cool evening breeze.

The scent of pine and the salty tang of the ocean mingled in the crisp July air as I stepped out of my cabin in Juneau, ready for the Fourth of July festivities. The sky was a brilliant blue, dotted with fluffy white clouds that seemed to dance with the spirit of the holiday. Excitement buzzed in the air, and I could hear the distant sound of music and laughter echoing through the streets.

I joined my friends, Cassie and Sarah, at the edge of the main road, where the parade would soon kick off. The vibrant colors of red, white, and blue decorated the storefronts, and a sea of people gathered, some waving small flags, others wearing star-spangled hats. It was a small-town celebration, but the energy felt electric.

"Can you believe we're finally here?" Cassie exclaimed, her eyes sparkling with excitement. She wore a bright red sundress that swayed with every movement, and I admired how effortlessly she captured the festive spirit.

"Honestly, it feels like a scene from a movie," I said, smiling at the children running around with cotton candy and balloons. The anticipation hung thick in the air, a palpable sense of community that warmed my heart.

Sarah nudged us playfully. "Okay, ladies, get your cameras ready. We're going to capture every moment!" She was already holding her phone, poised to take photos, her grin infectious.

As the parade began, the sound of marching bands filled the air, and we cheered as colorful floats rolled by, each one more elaborate than the last. Local businesses showcased their pride with decorated trucks and kids waving from the back, laughter echoing around us. I couldn't help but laugh at the sight of a float adorned with a giant fishing net, where children pretended to fish while dressed in comical oversized boots.

"This is everything I hoped it would be," I said, glancing at my friends as we clapped for the participants. They were fully immersed in the celebration, and I felt a wave of gratitude wash over me. It was moments like these that reminded me of the beauty in small-town life, the sense of belonging that came with it.

The parade continued, with veterans riding in convertibles and waving to the crowd, their faces etched with pride and history. I felt a lump in my throat as I recognized the sacrifices they had made for our freedom. It was a reminder of the deeper significance behind the festivities.

As the last float passed, a hush fell over the crowd, a collective breath held in anticipation. "Are you ready for the fireworks?" Sarah asked, her voice barely above a whisper, excitement dancing in her eyes.

"Absolutely," I replied, feeling a thrill run through me.

* * *

The sky was painted in those last shades of pink and gold before nightfall, and I could already feel the excitement building as the city prepared for the fireworks.

Jack and I climbed up to the top deck, finding a spot where we could sit together with a clear view of the sky. As the sun sank below the horizon, the mountains rose around us in shadowy outlines, the air thick with the smell of saltwater and the distant scent of barbecues from boats nearby.

We didn't talk much as we waited. I was hyper-aware of his hand brushing against mine, of his shoulder pressing into mine. In the quiet, I felt the weight of our unspoken questions lingering, the ones that kept creeping back, even when I tried to push them down.

Just then, the first firework shot up, crackling in a dazzling burst of red and gold. I gasped as it lit up the sky, and Jack chuckled softly beside me.

"Pretty incredible, isn't it?" he murmured, his eyes fixed on the sky.

I nodded, letting the colors and sounds wash over me. The fireworks reflected off the water, and the echoes bounced off the mountains, amplifying the spectacle all around us. Each burst filled the harbor with color, lighting up the boats and faces of the people nearby. It felt like we were caught in a moment outside of time.

I glanced over at Jack, watching his face as he watched the fireworks, his eyes filled with quiet awe. I reached out and slipped my hand into his, feeling his fingers interlace with mine, warm and solid.

As the grand finale began, the fireworks filled the sky with brilliant explosions, one after another, until it felt like the world was filled with light. I turned to Jack, catching his gaze in the glow of the colors reflecting off his face. He looked at me with a softness that made my heart ache.

Without a word, he leaned closer, and I felt his lips brush against mine. I closed my eyes, sinking into the kiss, feeling the warmth of him as the fireworks exploded around us, filling the sky and the air with sound and light. The world around us disappeared until there was just him, his hands cupping my face, his touch steady and grounding.

When we finally broke apart, breathless, I kept my eyes closed, memorizing the feeling of this moment—the fireworks, the mountains, the echoing sound, and Jack, right here with me.

As the final sparks fizzled out and the sky turned dark, I opened my eyes and met his gaze. Neither of us said anything, but the questions and worries faded, at least for a moment. In this place, surrounded by the beauty of Alaska and the glow of fireworks, it felt like anything was possible.

* * *

The next morning, as the boat swayed gently in the harbor, I sat in the small lounge area with Sarah and Cassie, the sounds of clinking coffee mugs and soft murmurs of other passengers around us. Jack had gone to the dock to check on some final details of our departure, so it was just the three of us, finally in a quiet moment.

Sarah nudged me with her elbow. "So," she started, her eyes sparkling. "Are you going to tell us what's really going on with you and Jack?"

My face flushed instantly. "What do you mean?"

"Oh, come on," Cassie said, grinning. "It's so obvious, Mackenzie! I've never seen you look at someone like that."

I bit my lip, a small smile creeping onto my face despite myself. "Alright, fine," I admitted, looking down at my coffee. "Something has been... happening. We've spent so much time together on this trip, and last night, during the fireworks..." I trailed off, letting the memory of Jack's kiss play out in my mind.

Sarah gasped, clasping her hands together. "You kissed during the grand finale? Mackenzie, that's literally out of a romance novel."

Cassie leaned forward, her eyes widening. "So what happens now? Are you two going to try long-distance?"

I sighed, running a hand through my hair. "I don't know," I admitted. "He lives here in Alaska, his work, his life... it's all here. And I'm back in New York. I've thought about long-distance, but it seems like such a huge leap. We'd both be trying to manage different schedules, and honestly, I'm afraid it won't work. I don't want to risk getting hurt—or hurting him."

Sarah put a reassuring hand on my shoulder. "I get it, Mackenzie. It's scary, but you have something special with him. You've been happier this week than I've seen you in a long time."

"Plus," Cassie added, her voice gentle, "maybe trying long-distance is worth it. Just to see if it could work. You don't have to make a lifelong decision right now. Just... start with staying in touch, visiting each other. See how it feels."

I nodded slowly, letting their words sink in. "You're both right. Maybe I owe it to myself—and to him to try. If it's this hard to let go now, maybe that's saying something."

Sarah squeezed my hand. "You can figure it out, Mackenzie. Even if it's messy and complicated, it could be worth it. Just take it one step at a time."

I looked out the window at the mountains, at the place I'd come to love over the past few days. The idea of leaving Jack here tugged at my heart, but the idea of giving up on whatever we were building tugged even harder.

"Alright," I said finally, taking a deep breath. "I'm going to talk to him. We'll see if we can make this work."

11

The day of my departure crept up too fast. One minute, I was caught up in the magic of Alaska, and the next, I was packing my suitcase, knowing this goodbye with Jack was looming. Sarah and Cassie had already left for the airport, giving Jack and I some space that I much appreciated. As we walked down to the harbor together, the quiet between us held so many unspoken things.

We reached the dock where my taxi would soon arrive, and Jack finally turned to me, his hands stuffed deep into his jacket pockets. The morning air was cool, the gray-blue mountains rising behind him like a silent witness to everything we weren't saying.

"Mack... My Mackerel," he began softly, his voice carrying that same weight I'd been feeling all morning. "I... I've been thinking about this a lot, about us." His gaze dropped to the wooden planks beneath our feet. "And as much as I want this, want you... I don't think I can do long-distance."

My heart sank, though I'd known deep down this was coming. "I understand," I whispered, trying to keep my voice steady. "It's a lot to ask. We both have our own lives, and it's not fair to either of us to keep trying to bridge the gap."

He looked up, his eyes shining with that familiar warmth but shadowed by something deeper—pain, maybe regret. "It doesn't change how I feel about you. None of this does. But... I just don't know how to make it work with me here and you there."

I swallowed, feeling tears welling up in my eyes. "I get it, Jack. Really, I do." A tear slipped down my cheek, and he reached out, brushing it away, his fingers lingering just a moment too long.

He pulled me into a tight embrace, and I let myself sink into him, pressing my face against his chest, memorizing the steady rhythm of his heartbeat. His arms wrapped around me as though he didn't want to let go, and maybe that was the hardest part—knowing that even though we didn't want this to end, it had to.

"I wouldn't trade any of it," I whispered, pulling back enough to look up at him. "Every moment, every hike, every conversation... I don't regret any of it. I'm glad we had this time together, even if it has to end."

His lips curved into a sad smile, and he brushed a loose strand of hair behind my ear. "Me too," he said quietly. "I don't think I'll ever forget this week. Or you."

The distant hum of the taxi's engine grew louder, signaling that our time was running out. I squeezed his hand, taking one last look at the mountains, the harbor, and finally, Jack—the man who'd made this place feel like home in such a short time.

As the cab pulled in, we stepped apart. "Goodbye, Jack," I murmured, my voice breaking.

He held my gaze, his own eyes shimmering with unshed tears. "Goodbye, Mackenzie."

I turned and walked up the ramp, feeling the sharp sting of each step away from him. As I got into the car, I looked back to see him standing there, hands in his pockets, watching as the boat pulled away. I lifted a hand, and he lifted his in return, a silent goodbye that echoed in my heart long after the shoreline disappeared.

And though it hurt to leave, I knew these two weeks would stay with me forever. Alaska had changed me, and Jack had been a part of that. No matter what the future held, I knew I'd never forget him—or what we'd shared.

* * *

As the plane soared above the mountains and glaciers of Alaska, I leaned back in my seat, the weight of the past few days settling into my chest. I couldn't take my eyes off the view outside—the jagged peaks and stretches of untouched forest below. Soon, this place would be just a memory.

Cassie and Sarah, sitting beside me, had been quiet since takeoff, probably sensing that something was on my mind. Eventually, Cassie nudged me, breaking the silence.

"Alright, Mackenzie," she said softly, her gaze gentle but curious. "What happened with Jack? We know something did. You've barely spoken since we left the harbor."

I hesitated, staring out the window for a second before I turned back to them, the ache of it all rising to the surface. "We said goodbye. For good."

Sarah's face softened immediately. "Oh, Mackenzie..."

I managed a small smile, trying to keep my voice steady. "He... he doesn't want to try long distance. He doesn't think it would work with me in New York and him here."

Cassie's mouth opened in shock, and she exchanged a quick glance with Sarah. "Did you tell him how you felt? That you'd be open to trying?"

I nodded, letting out a shaky breath. "Yeah, I did. I told him that being with him meant more to me than he probably realized, but... he was set on it. He thinks he's making the right choice. And honestly, I can understand where he's coming from."

They both watched me, faces full of sympathy, before Sarah reached over to give my hand a reassuring squeeze. "But, Mackenzie... long distance can work. Plenty of people do it."

"I know," I replied, my voice barely a whisper. "But Jack doesn't think we'd be able to handle it, not with his life here and mine back home. And maybe he's right. Maybe it'd just hurt too much, trying to bridge this gap between us when we barely know what the future holds."

Sarah's brows furrowed as she looked at me thoughtfully. "But maybe it's worth trying, even with all the unknowns."

I looked down, my heart caught between the idea of holding on to something so incredible and letting go. "Part of me thinks that, too," I admitted. "But I know Jack was serious when he said goodbye. And... maybe he has a point. We both have our own lives and our own dreams. Asking him to leave Alaska, or thinking about me moving here someday, it feels like more than we could realistically hope for right now."

Cassie leaned her head back against the seat, looking at me with the softest expression. "But that doesn't mean this connection wasn't real. You obviously meant something to each other—sometimes, just that can be enough. You don't have to know the end result right now."

I swallowed, nodding as I tried to hold back tears. "Yeah. That's what I told him when we said goodbye. That I didn't regret a single second with him. I just... wish there were more to have."

The three of us fell into silence, the hum of the plane filling the air as I tried to process everything. Being with Jack had felt like discovering a missing piece of myself, one I never even knew I needed. And now, leaving that behind, it felt like letting go of something I hadn't even fully experienced yet.

After a while, Sarah's voice pulled me out of my thoughts. "Mackenzie, I know it hurts now. But if this is really meant to be, maybe you and Jack will find your way back to each other someday."

I managed a small smile, her words offering a flicker of hope I hadn't expected. "Maybe," I whispered, resting my head back against the seat, feeling the exhaustion of the trip and of goodbye settle in.

And as the plane carried us further from Alaska, I let myself take one last look out the window, the mountains slowly fading from view. Whatever happened next, I knew this place—and Jack—would always be a part of me.

* * *

Back in New York, I settled into my usual corner of the coffee shop, the chatter of patrons and the hum of the espresso machine blending into a comfortable background noise. I opened my laptop, the blank document staring back at me as if it knew I wasn't quite ready to dive in. The memories of Alaska felt so close, so vivid, that I could almost feel the chill of the ocean air and hear the echo of fireworks off the mountains. My fingers hovered over the keyboard, and then I started to type.

The words came slowly at first, like walking barefoot into a cold stream, but gradually, they began to flow. I wrote about the boat, the endless waves surrounding us, and how every morning had felt like waking up in a new world. I described Funter Bay, the cliffside rocks we climbed, the buoy swing Jack and I had jumped from, laughing and gasping as we plunged into the icy water. Those days felt more vibrant than any I'd ever experienced.

Then I wrote about Cinnamon Island, and my chest tightened a little as I described how Jack had shown it to me, his face alight with a boyish grin, proud and eager to share a place so dear to him. I could still feel the warmth of the sun that day, the smell of salt and pine in the air. And I wrote about our picnic there—his laughter, the way he'd watched me with a softness I hadn't expected, the shared silence that had meant more than any words.

I took a sip of my coffee, feeling that ache of longing again. But I pressed on. I wrote about the Fourth of July fireworks, the way the bursts of color had lit up the sky and Jack had taken my hand, his face illuminated by the glow. I couldn't stop the bittersweet smile that formed as I relived our last night together. Just for a moment, in the grand finale, I'd let myself believe that it could all somehow work out.

When I finally got to our goodbye, I paused, my fingers stilled over the keyboard. Writing about it made the memory feel sharp again, the ache just as fresh. I thought about his face as he'd told me he couldn't do long distance, the sadness in his eyes matching my own. I hadn't wanted to let go, and I knew he hadn't either. But he'd made his choice, and I'd respected it, no matter how much it hurt.

After a deep breath, I typed out our parting words, the moment we'd shared one last look, knowing it was the end. My eyes stung as I wrote, but I reminded myself that this was part of my story. Our story. Alaska wasn't just a place I'd visited—it was an experience that had changed me, that had shown me new sides of myself and awakened dreams I hadn't known I was carrying.

Hours slipped by, and the coffee shop around me grew quieter as the day moved on. I added every detail, every feeling, letting myself pour it all onto the page. By the time I finished, a sense of peace settled over me, mingling with the ache that still lingered. Maybe I'd never see Jack again, but writing this felt like keeping a piece of him close. In sharing our story, I could relive those precious moments and keep them safe.

Closing my laptop, I sat back, feeling both exhausted and lighter somehow. Alaska might be miles away, but in these pages, I knew it would stay with me always.

* * *

After finishing the last chapter, I sat staring at the document on my screen, a nervous thrill pulsing through me. The entire trip to Alaska, every memory, every feeling, every last moment with Jack—each of them now lived in the pages of this manuscript. It felt more like a diary than a book, a private story meant only for me.

But, with a deep breath, I opened my email and attached the document. My other editor, Lila, had been waiting eagerly, already texting me for updates, knowing I was close to finishing. I typed out a quick message—"Here it is, all finished! It's very personal, though, so I'm not sure yet if it's ready for the world..."—and pressed send before I could overthink it.

Two days later, my phone buzzed with a message from Lila: *"Just finished reading. Call me as soon as you can. This is amazing."*

My heart jumped, and I dialed her number immediately. Lila answered on the first ring, and I could practically feel her excitement radiating through the phone.

"Mackenzie, this is beautiful," she gushed, her voice filled with warmth. "I mean, I knew you could write, but this... there's such rawness, such honesty. It's so vivid I felt like I was right there with you."

I let out a shaky laugh, surprised and flattered. "You really think it's that good?"

"It's not just good, Mackenzie—it's powerful. I can see this resonating with so many people. The descriptions, the emotions, the sense of discovery... it's all so alive." She paused, her tone growing softer. "But, I can tell it's personal. You don't have to publish if it feels too vulnerable. This could just be for you."

I took a deep breath, staring out my apartment window, feeling a rush of mixed emotions. There was a part of me that wanted to hold these memories close, to keep them as something just for me. I thought about Jack, about our time together and how much he meant to me, how he'd shaped the story of my time in Alaska. It felt like putting him—and us—on display. But another part of me, the part that Lila's words encouraged, felt that maybe sharing this could be healing. Not just for me, but maybe for others, too.

"I don't know, Lila," I admitted. "It's one thing to write it, but it's another to let the whole world in on something so close to my heart. I mean, I've never even written about my life like this before."

"I get it. It's a risk, and it's scary," she replied. "But sometimes those are the stories that people need the most. The real ones. That's what's so beautiful about this book—it's not just Alaska, it's about all the emotions, all the discovery, the loss, and growth. It's about love and adventure and letting go, and that's something so many people will connect with. But it's entirely up to you. Take your time deciding."

We talked a little more, her encouragement softening my initial doubts. By the time we hung up, I felt both grounded and a bit more open to the idea. Maybe sharing this story didn't mean letting go of my memories with Jack. Maybe, in some way, publishing it would mean honoring them.

As I closed my laptop and sank back into my couch, I took a deep breath. I'd written my heart out, that much I knew. Now I just had to decide if I was ready to share it with the world.

12

*P*resent Day*

Five years had passed since that summer in Alaska, yet there were moments when it felt like only yesterday. I sat at my desk, the light of the late afternoon sun pouring through the window, casting a warm glow over the scattered pages of my latest manuscript. The city buzzed outside, but my mind wandered to a different place entirely.

I could picture the rugged landscape of Alaska—the towering mountains, the deep blue of the glacial waters, and the way the sunlight danced on the surface. Most vividly, I recalled Jack's laughter, the way it seemed to echo off the mountains surrounding us. I found myself leaning back in my chair, closing my eyes to savor the memories.

That summer had been transformative. I had gone to Alaska with my friends, seeking adventure and inspiration for my writing, but I left with something I hadn't expected: a deep connection to Jack. I could still hear his voice, see the warmth in his blue eyes when he looked at me, and feel the way he made the world seem bigger and brighter.

The first time I had seen him, perched on that old fishing boat, his hair tousled by the wind, I knew I was in for something special. Our days spent kayaking to Cinnamon Island, laughing as we splashed each other with water, and lying on the beach talking about our dreams felt like pages from a novel I wished I could write. But it was our quiet moments, the ones where he looked at me with an intensity that made the rest of the world fade away, that lingered in my mind the most.

Yet, as much as I loved those memories, they were bittersweet. I had poured my heart into my writing since I returned, crafting stories that were both inspired by and infused with the emotions of that summer. It was cathartic but also challenging to write about the love I'd felt for Jack, knowing that the reality of our lives had pulled us in different directions. I could still hear the last words he had said to me as we stood on the dock, saying goodbye for what felt like the last time. I had watched him walk away, my heart aching with the weight of everything we'd shared.

As I typed away at my keyboard, I couldn't help but wonder if he thought about me too. Did he ever look up at the Alaskan sky and remember the fireworks we had watched on that final night? Did he miss our late-night talks and the way we had dreamt about our futures, even if we both knew they might not align?

I paused, staring at the blinking cursor on the screen, my thoughts drifting back to the stories I had spun over the years. I had been fortunate to have success as a writer, but something about the upcoming anniversary of my trip made me hesitate. The words flowed easily when I wrote about the adventure, but as I delved into the emotions surrounding my time with Jack, I became apprehensive. The memories felt too raw, too personal, as if revealing them would somehow expose the parts of me that were still tender from that goodbye.

With a sigh, I turned away from the screen and poured myself a cup of coffee. I needed clarity. I thought about reaching out to my friends, Sarah and Cassie, who had shared that summer with me. They were always a source of wisdom, and perhaps they could help me figure out how to reconcile my past with my present.

As I dialed Sarah's number, I felt a familiar flutter of nerves in my stomach. When she picked up, her voice was warm and inviting. "Hey, Mackenzie! How's it going?"

"Hey! I've been working on rewriting my book, but I'm feeling a bit stuck," I admitted. "I've been thinking a lot about Alaska... about Jack."

There was a pause on the line. "Oh, wow. That was a pivotal time for you. How are you feeling about it?"

"Conflicted, I guess. I want to capture that summer, but it feels so personal. I'm not sure if I want to put all those emotions out into the world," I confessed.

Sarah was quiet for a moment, and I could almost hear her considering her words. "Mackenzie, your experiences are what make your writing special. You don't have to publish it if it doesn't feel right, but if you're afraid to share it, maybe there's something really powerful there that others could connect with."

I nodded, even though she couldn't see me. "You think so?"

"I know so. Just think about how much that summer meant to you. If you can share that, it might help someone else who's been through a similar situation," she encouraged.

"I just... I want to do it justice. I want to honor what Jack and I had, even if it's not perfect," I replied, my heart racing at the thought of diving back into those memories.

"Then do it. Take your time with it, and write it for you first. The rest will follow," Sarah said firmly.

After we hung up, I felt a surge of determination. I returned to my desk and stared at the blank document in front of me, my fingers hovering above the keys. I took a deep breath, feeling the weight of both nostalgia and excitement. I wanted to finish writing about the beauty of that summer, the lessons learned, and the love I had found in the most unexpected place.

With that thought in mind, I began to type, letting the final words flow as the memories of Jack and Alaska poured out of me. I embraced the uncertainty, knowing that the journey of writing about my past was as important as the experiences themselves. And perhaps, just perhaps, it would lead me to the next chapter of my life, wherever that might be.

* * *

Sitting at the small, dimly lit table in the corner of a bustling restaurant, I couldn't help but feel a wave of anxiety wash over me. I glanced around, my gaze flickering between the twinkling lights overhead and the couples laughing together. My heart raced slightly as I awaited my blind date, a setup arranged by Cassie, who was always trying to nudge me toward new experiences.

When I'd told her I was ready to get back into dating, I hadn't envisioned a blind date. My last relationship—if you could call it that—was an undeniable connection that left me wondering if I'd ever feel that spark again. Jack had ignited something in me that felt rare, and I hadn't quite managed to extinguish the flame.

I glanced at my watch, then back at the door. Maybe this was a mistake. Just as I contemplated slipping out the back, a tall man entered the restaurant, scanning the room. He wore a navy blue blazer over a crisp white shirt and seemed confident as he strode toward me. I offered a polite smile as he approached.

"Hey! You must be Mackenzie," he said, extending his hand with an easy grin.

"Yep, that's me," I replied, shaking his hand. "Nice to meet you, uh..."

"Evan," he said, taking a seat across from me. "I'm really glad we could meet up. Cassie had some great things to say about you."

I nodded, forcing a smile as I settled into my chair. I wanted to be open-minded and give this a chance, but my heart wasn't really in it. The waiter arrived, and I ordered a glass of wine, hoping it would help ease my nerves. Evan ordered a burger and fries, which seemed fittingly casual for our setting.

"So, what do you do for fun?" he asked, leaning back in his chair, clearly trying to engage me in conversation.

I took a sip of my wine, considering my response. "I'm a writer, mostly. I love creating stories and immersing myself in different worlds."

"Oh, cool! What do you write about?" he asked, his interest seemingly genuine.

I hesitated, thinking about how to summarize the whirlwind of emotions and experiences I'd captured in my recent work. "A little bit of everything, really. I've been focusing on some personal stories lately."

Evan nodded, but I could see his attention waning. I tried to push through, sharing snippets about my recent writing journey, but he quickly redirected the conversation toward himself, talking about his job in finance and the recent promotion he had received.

As he rambled on about numbers and projections, I felt my mind drifting. My thoughts were back in Alaska, where everything had felt so vibrant and alive. I remembered the way Jack's laughter had filled the air, how every conversation had felt charged with an electric energy that was now glaringly absent.

"...and then we had a team-building exercise that turned into a drinking game. It was hilarious!" Evan finished, grinning widely.

I forced a laugh, but it felt hollow. "That sounds fun." The words felt insipid as they left my lips.

"So, do you like to travel?" Evan asked, shifting the conversation back to a safer topic.

"Definitely. I just got back from Alaska, actually," I replied, hoping to stir something deeper in our exchange.

"Alaska, huh? That sounds cold," he said, chuckling as if the mere thought of it was preposterous.

I felt a pang of irritation. "It's actually beautiful. The landscape is breathtaking. I went kayaking, hiking, and even went on a floatplane. The whole trip was incredible."

"Wow, sounds intense," he said, his eyes drifting to the side as if he was more interested in the couple behind me than in my story. "I'm more of a beach person myself. I'd rather be somewhere warm, you know?"

The disconnect felt more pronounced in that moment. I wanted to dive deeper into the magic of Alaska, to share the way the mountains had felt like they were cradling my heart, how the sunsets painted the sky in shades of pink and gold, and how Jack had made everything feel possible. But I could see it in Evan's eyes—he wasn't interested in those details.

The conversation continued, but each moment felt like a struggle. I made small talk and nodded along, but it was as if we were speaking different languages. I glanced around the restaurant, the laughter and clinking of glasses surrounding us, but I felt utterly alone.

Finally, after what felt like an eternity, Evan checked his watch. "I should probably get going soon. I have a big meeting in the morning," he said, a hint of relief in his voice.

"Yeah, of course," I replied, my heart sinking. The evening hadn't exactly gone as I'd hoped.

We finished our drinks, and I made a half-hearted attempt to salvage the date. "It was nice to meet you," I said, trying to summon some enthusiasm.

"Yeah, you too. We should do this again sometime," he said, but there was a casualness to his tone that made me doubt his sincerity.

"Sure," I replied, even though I knew I wouldn't reach out.

As we stood to leave, I felt a sense of closure, though not the kind I had hoped for. The night air was cool as we stepped outside, and I took a deep breath, savoring the familiar city scents. I couldn't help but compare this experience to my time with Jack, where every moment had felt precious, like the hours we spent talking under the stars, dreaming about our futures.

"Take care, Mackenzie," Evan said, offering a wave before walking away.

I turned, watching him disappear into the crowd, and for the first time that night, I felt the weight of my own heart. I missed the connection, the excitement, and the undeniable chemistry that had felt so effortless with Jack. I was still haunted by what could have been, and I wondered if I would ever feel that spark again.

With a sigh, I made my way to the subway, knowing that I needed to keep moving forward. But as I sat on the train, I couldn't shake the feeling that I was searching for something—or someone—who could make my heart race the way Jack had. It was a hard truth to accept, but maybe I needed to embrace the journey ahead, even if it was paved with memories that were hard to let go of.

* * *

I met up with Sarah for coffee the next day, the blind date still lingering in the back of my mind. She'd been excited for me to go on this date, hoping it might finally be something real, something lasting.

"So, how did it go?" she asked, leaning forward with a grin, her coffee mug in hand.

I hesitated, swirling my own mug. "It was... okay. He was nice. We had a good conversation, and he was interesting. It just... it wasn't a strong connection, you know?"

She nodded, her grin fading into a more understanding expression. "Like, you were there, but it didn't quite click the way you hoped?"

"Exactly. I don't know, maybe I'm being too picky, but I keep thinking about how it felt with Jack. Even though we had our own set of challenges, that connection was undeniable. It's hard not to compare, and I know it's not fair to anyone new."

Sarah gave a sympathetic smile, reaching over to pat my hand. "I get it. And hey, maybe you're not being too picky. It's natural to want something that feels... like that. But don't worry—just because you haven't felt it with anyone else yet doesn't mean you never will."

I smiled back, appreciating her encouragement. "I know. I just want to be able to let go and move on, but sometimes I wonder if I'm holding onto something that's never going to come around again."

She shook her head. "Don't think of it that way. Just take it one day, one person at a time. And who knows? Maybe the best part of your love story is still waiting to be written."

Her words lingered, and as we talked about other things, I tried to convince myself she might be right.

13

I pushed open the door to my cabin, feeling the stillness settle in as I shrugged off my rain jacket, hanging it on the peg by the door. The evening was quiet, the sky faintly lit with the last traces of twilight, and outside, I could hear the gentle lap of waves against the dock. For the past five years, life here in Alaska had stayed the same—a steady rhythm of long days on the water, rough winters, and quiet nights just like this. And yet tonight, my mind drifted somewhere else. Somewhere back in time.

Meeting Mackenzie was like a flame sparking in the middle of the familiar, steady burn of my life here. She showed up that summer, wide-eyed and full of wonder, along with her friends, eager to see the wild parts of Alaska that I'd long called home. Her curiosity was contagious; there was something about her that made me feel... alive. It wasn't just her laugh or the way she'd look at me like she really saw me. It was how she looked at the world, with this openness, like she wasn't afraid to chase whatever called to her.

I never told anyone how much I'd thought about her after she left. But the truth is, she was always there in my mind, popping up whenever I let myself wonder what life might look like beyond this place.

Life here has been good, no complaints. I've met plenty of people since, mostly travelers passing through, curious about "real Alaska." But none of them really got it, not like she did. Most of them weren't ready to stay or adapt to this kind of life. It didn't take long to figure that out.

And lately, my family and friends have been on me more than usual. "When are you gonna find someone who'll stick around?" they ask, or "Don't you ever think about settling down?" I laugh it off, but their questions dig a little deeper each time. For a while, I could push it aside. Now? Now, I'm not so sure.

I poured a cup of coffee, watching the steam rise as the water outside turned dusky and gray. Even with everything I've built here—the business, the life I'm proud of—there's this feeling I can't shake. Like maybe something's missing.

Maybe that's why I can't stop thinking about her, five years later. I told myself I'd let go, that I wouldn't hold onto the past, but it's hard to forget how it felt to be with her. I wonder sometimes if she thinks about me too, if she ever feels the pull to come back.

** * **

The boat rocked under my feet as I got the fishing lines ready, the early morning air carrying a mix of salt and pine. The sun was still fighting through a layer of mist over the water, and I looked up as the group I was guiding gathered near the bow, chatting excitedly and snapping photos of the mountains behind us.

One of them—a blonde with sunglasses perched on her head—wandered over, smiling easily. "So, Jack," she said, drawing out my name in a teasing tone. "Do you ever get tired of all this beauty?"

I chuckled, shrugging as I adjusted the tackle. "Can't say that I do," I replied, glancing out at the water. "Every day's different out here."

She exchanged a look with her friend, who nudged her with a grin, like she was urging her on. She leaned in, her smile widening. "I bet a local guy like you has all kinds of stories," she said, tilting her head. "How does someone end up doing this? Running a boat, taking people out here every day?"

I felt that familiar awkwardness settle in, but I kept my tone light. "Grew up around it. Hard not to want to stay when you've got a view like this every morning."

She laughed, waiting for more. "I guess I can see that," she said, lingering a little too long. "But I bet you meet all kinds of people. Ever take a break from the Alaskan wilderness to visit somewhere exciting?"

I shook my head, giving her a polite but final answer. "Not too often," I said simply. "This keeps me busy enough." I turned back to the line, the subtle shift in my tone making it clear I was done with the conversation.

She hesitated, then let out a small, disappointed laugh before heading back to her friends. I heard them murmuring, one of them glancing back at me with a giggle. I forced a polite smile, but I could feel myself stiffening. I used to be more open to this kind of chat, maybe even flirt a bit if it felt right. Lately, though, I didn't have much patience for it. None of it was what I wanted.

My thoughts wandered, unbidden, back to Mackenzie. No one I'd met since had come close to sparking the same feeling, let alone making me feel like I could actually let them in. With her, I'd felt... free, like she saw this place and me exactly for what we were, no need to change a thing.

I let out a slow breath, straightening up as I looked out over the water. There were still a few minutes until we'd start casting lines, so I stood at the edge of the boat, taking it all in—the mountains in the distance, the endless stretch of ocean, the quiet pulse of waves against the hull. It was everything I loved, everything that had always felt like home.

But more and more, I was starting to wonder if it was enough.

* * *

I dipped the paddle into the water, pushing myself slowly away from the shore as the early evening light softened, casting a warm glow over the bay. I hadn't paddled out to Cinnamon Island on my own in months, maybe even longer. This used to be my place to think, to clear my mind, but tonight it felt different. There was a weight in my chest I couldn't ignore, a heaviness that hadn't been there when I first started coming out here.

The water was smooth, barely a ripple around me as I maneuvered the kayak toward the little island. As I got closer, the familiar rocky outcrop came into view, along with the narrow strip of sandy beach. I could almost see her there, laughing as she tried to scramble up the rocks that first time. She'd looked so out of place and at home all at once—like she belonged here, even though she was just passing through.

I couldn't help but smile to myself as I secured the kayak and stepped onto the shore, scanning the place like I half-expected to find her waiting here. It was strange to think that five years had slipped by since that summer. And yet, she was still here, lingering in every corner of this place. Cinnamon Island hadn't changed at all; the little beach, the rocks—they felt untouched, timeless in a way that made those memories feel close, almost real, as if I'd see her shadow around any corner.

I found my favorite spot on the rocks and sat down, looking out over the water, listening to the distant call of a seabird and the quiet rush of waves against the stones. Back then, I'd been so sure that somehow, someday, I'd see her again. That she'd find her way back. But time has a funny way of slipping past, and now I don't know if that's even possible. She's out there in New York, building the life she dreamed of, no doubt thriving. And here I am, right where she left me.

I ran my hand over the weathered rock beside me, a mix of bittersweet memories tugging at me. She'd understood what this place meant, how it kept me grounded, the peace it brought. I hadn't known how much I needed that feeling until I saw her appreciate it too, the way she took in Alaska with wide eyes and a deep breath, like she could feel its pull as strongly as I did.

I closed my eyes, letting the sound of the water wash over me. She was the one person who had seen me completely, without me having to explain anything. And that thought was as comforting as it was painful. I could see her here so clearly—her laughter echoing across the water, her eyes bright with wonder at the simplicity of it all.

As the light dimmed, I let the silence settle in, trying to accept that maybe this was all we'd ever have—memories, flashes of a connection that still held me, even after all these years. A part of me had always hoped she'd come back, or maybe that I'd find a way to reach her somehow. But life didn't play out that way, and now I'm not even sure how to bridge the distance, even if she wanted me to.

With a sigh, I stood up, taking one last look around. Cinnamon Island still held its magic, but I couldn't help but wonder if it was time to find something that wasn't just a memory. Something that could bring me that same spark, that same wonder, here in the life I've made.

* * *

The morning sun was just beginning to warm the dock as I guided my cousins onto the Northern Light. They'd come up from the Lower 48 for a long-overdue visit, and I could practically feel their excitement radiating as they climbed aboard, their eyes wide with wonder at the boat and the vast expanse of water stretching beyond the harbor.

"I can't believe you get to call this your office," my cousin Tyler said, clapping me on the back. "I knew you had it good up here, but this is insane."

I chuckled, shaking my head. "Not a bad setup, huh? Let's see if I can make it live up to the hype."

As we shoved off, the engine hummed beneath us, and I felt the familiar thrill of pulling away from the dock, the boat swaying gently beneath my feet. I leaned into the helm, watching the landmarks slip by while glancing back at my cousins. They were already snapping photos, their faces lit up with awe as they pointed out mountains and fishing boats in the distance.

"So, what's on the agenda today, Captain?" Ava asked, grinning as she leaned over the side of the boat, watching the wake we were leaving behind.

"I figured we'd hit a few good spots, see some wildlife, maybe try our hand at fishing if you're up for it," I replied, easing the boat into a smooth glide. "There's a chance we'll spot some humpbacks this time of year, maybe even some sea lions if we're lucky."

"Sounds perfect," Tyler said, pulling out a thermos from his backpack and pouring a round of coffee for everyone. "Here's to life in Alaska," he said, raising his cup.

"To Alaska," we echoed, clinking our mugs together.

As we moved farther from shore, I pointed out a rocky inlet where bald eagles were known to nest and navigated toward a small cove where I'd seen humpback whales breaching just the week before. I could see the anticipation in my cousins' faces as they scanned the water, eager for any sign of movement.

"Hey, look—over there!" Ava shouted, pointing toward a ripple in the water a few hundred yards off.

We all watched in awe as a humpback surfaced, its massive, graceful back rising above the water before it dove again, leaving only a trail of bubbles behind. I felt a thrill of pride and satisfaction as I took in my cousins' reactions—their pure wonder at seeing something so majestic up close.

"That never gets old," I murmured, more to myself than anyone else. Moments like this reminded me why I'd chosen this life—why I'd stayed here in Alaska, year after year.

After a while, we anchored near a small, secluded island I knew well. I pulled out the fishing gear, and my cousins eagerly took their spots at the side of the boat, casting their lines with a mix of determination and hopeful excitement.

"Any tips for rookies?" Tyler asked, adjusting his grip on the rod.

"Patience is key. And if you feel a tug, don't yank too hard. Let it play out," I said, my tone light as I settled into my own spot.

Before long, Tyler felt a bite and managed to reel in a decent-sized halibut, his grin stretching from ear to ear as I helped him pull it aboard. Ava caught one shortly after, and we both cheered as they held up their catches for a photo.

As the day wore on, my cousins relaxed into the rhythm of the boat, swapping stories and laughing at old family memories, all while asking me about the intricacies of life up north. I felt a rare contentment, the kind I'd only really known out here on the water. I hadn't seen my cousins in years, but having them here, sharing this experience, reminded me of the importance of family and the power of shared adventures.

Standing at the edge of the Northern Light's top deck, we peered down at the shimmering, icy water below. A light breeze chilled the air, and despite the warm summer sun, I knew the water would be cold enough to take our breath away.

Ava crossed her arms, looking a bit nervous as she watched the gentle waves lap against the hull. "You're really serious about this?"

I laughed. "What's the matter, city folks? Too cold for you?"

Tyler rolled his eyes, trying to put on a brave face. "I've swum in colder...I think." But even he looked doubtful as he gazed at the deep blue below.

"Alright, here's the deal. We all go together, no chickening out," I said, positioning myself at the edge, feeling that familiar thrill of the jump build in my chest. "On three."

"Wait, wait—" Ava sputtered, but it was too late. I was already counting down.

"One... two... three!"

With a shout, I launched myself off the edge, plunging feet-first into the water. The cold enveloped me instantly, shocking my system, but I resurfaced with a whoop just as Tyler and Ava splashed down beside me. They both came up gasping and sputtering, but their laughter echoed across the water.

"Holy... that's freezing!" Tyler managed between shivers, laughing so hard he could barely keep his head above water.

"Nothing like a quick wake-up call," I grinned, treading water easily as I took in their wide-eyed, waterlogged expressions.

"Why didn't we do this sooner?" Ava laughed, her teeth chattering as she kicked her legs.

"Come on, we're going for a lap around the boat. Swim it out—keeps you warm," I said, already propelling myself forward with strong strokes.

They followed, swimming through the cold, invigorating water, rounding the stern with the boat's name painted proudly on its side. I glanced over, catching my cousins' exhilarated expressions as we swam alongside each other. Moments like these—spontaneous and slightly reckless—were what Alaska was all about.

As we circled back to the boat's ladder, Ava pulled herself up, shivering and breathless but grinning like a kid. Tyler followed, just as thrilled, water streaming from his hair as he collapsed onto the deck, still laughing.

I hauled myself up last, feeling that familiar pulse of warmth surge back as I toweled off. I moved quickly to the small galley and filled three mugs with hot cocoa, steam rising in inviting wisps.

"Hot chocolate to the rescue," I said, passing a mug to each of them. They took the mugs gratefully, holding them close for warmth as they leaned back against the bench seats.

"Worth every second of freezing," Ava said, taking a long sip and sighing as the warmth settled into her bones.

Tyler grinned, his eyes still sparkling with adrenaline. "Best day of the trip, hands down."

I took a sip, savoring the way the cocoa chased away the last remnants of the cold. "Well, there's plenty more where that came from." I raised my mug in a toast, and they followed suit, our smiles all saying the same thing: we'd just made a memory that would last a lifetime.

As we made our way back to shore, Tyler leaned over, nodding toward the expanse of ocean stretched out in front of us. "I get it now," he said quietly. "Why you stayed here. There's something about this place...it just sticks with you."

I nodded, the weight of his words settling comfortably in my chest. "Yeah, it does." I smiled, knowing that moments like this—the open ocean, the thrill of the catch, the laughter shared with family—were what made Alaska feel like home.

* * *

The morning sun was bright as I helped my cousins load their bags into the car, the excitement of the past few days still buzzing in the air. It felt strange, knowing they were heading back to Seattle, back to their busy lives, while I'd be returning to the quiet of Alaska. I tried to shake off the heaviness settling in my chest as I zipped up Ava's suitcase.

"Thanks for an amazing trip, Jack," Tyler said, slapping me on the back. "You really showed us a good time."

"Yeah, it was unforgettable," Ava chimed in, giving me a quick hug. "We can't wait to come back. You have to show us more of this place."

I smiled, doing my best to hide the twinge of sadness I felt at their departure. "I'm glad you guys had fun. It was great to have you here."

Tyler hesitated for a moment, a serious look crossing his face. "Listen, you should really come visit us in Seattle in a few weeks. It's been too long since we've all been together, and I know you could use a change of scenery."

I raised an eyebrow, surprised by the invitation. "Really? I don't know... I'm kind of tied up with work right now."

"Come on, man! You can't keep using work as an excuse. You need to get out of Alaska every once in a while," Tyler urged, his enthusiasm contagious. "We'll show you the city, hit some of the best spots, and just hang out like old times."

Ava nodded eagerly. "You could use a little adventure beyond the boat and the mountains. It'd be fun!"

I hesitated, my mind racing through the logistics of it all. The thought of leaving Alaska, even for a little while, felt daunting. But the idea of spending time with them, of reconnecting and having fun, was tempting.

"Okay, maybe I'll consider it," I said, trying to sound nonchalant. "But you guys have to promise me that you won't just drag me to a bunch of tourist traps."

"Deal," Tyler grinned. "We'll make sure it's worth your while."

As they finished packing up, I felt a flicker of excitement. Maybe a trip to Seattle wouldn't be so bad after all. It would be nice to experience something different, to step out of my routine, even if just for a few days.

"Just let me know when you guys are free, and I'll figure it out," I said, feeling a smile break across my face.

"Perfect!" Ava exclaimed, giving me another hug. "We'll set it up and make sure you have a blast. Don't think you can back out now!"

As they climbed into the car, I waved goodbye, watching them pull away. I stood there for a moment, the quiet of the dock enveloping me again. The sun sparkled on the water, and

I felt a stir of anticipation mixed with uncertainty. Maybe a change of scenery was exactly what I needed.

14

I stared at the email on my screen, still trying to wrap my head around the invitation. Speaking at a writers conference—me? My heart raced as I reread the words, each one sinking in deeper. "We'd be thrilled to have you share your journey and insights on the craft," it said. I could hardly believe it; this was a significant opportunity.

The next few days flew by in a blur of excitement and anxiety. I jotted down notes, piecing together my thoughts on what I wanted to share. There were so many moments that shaped my writing, and I wanted to convey that to the audience, to inspire them in the same way I'd been inspired.

Packing was another adventure altogether. I rummaged through my closet, pulling out clothes that felt right. A simple yet professional blazer, a few blouses, and a comfortable pair of shoes—I had to be ready for anything, including long hours of standing and talking. I laid everything out on my bed, organizing it into a neat pile while glancing at my suitcase.

My mind wandered as I folded my clothes, thinking about how long it had been since I'd done something like this. The hustle and bustle of city life faded into the background, replaced by a sense of purpose. I was stepping into a new chapter, one where I could share my passion for storytelling with others.

I zipped up my suitcase and stood back, admiring my work. I took a moment to breathe, feeling the weight of anticipation settle on my shoulders. I was ready.

Once I was finished, I grabbed my bag and headed out the door. The fresh air greeted me as I stepped outside, and I could feel a nervous excitement buzzing in my veins. I hailed a cab, my heart racing as I thought about the journey ahead. This could be a pivotal moment for me, a chance to connect with other writers and maybe even find inspiration for my next project.

As the cab pulled away from the curb, I watched the familiar streets of New York blur by, each block a reminder of the life I'd built here. It felt strange leaving it all behind, even for a few days, but I welcomed the change. It was time to embrace new experiences, new connections, and new stories waiting to unfold.

The airport buzzed with life when I arrived. I maneuvered through the crowds, following the signs to my terminal. As I waited at the gate, I felt a mix of nerves and excitement. I pulled out my notebook, flipping to a blank page and jotting down a few key points for my talk.

Suddenly, it hit me: I was about to share my story with a room full of people who shared my passion. I couldn't wait. This was my moment, and I was ready to seize it.

* * *

As I navigated the bustling Seattle airport, anticipation tingled in my fingertips. The Writers Conference was just around the corner, and I was eager to dive into workshops, soak up knowledge, and connect with fellow writers. After a long flight from New York, I couldn't wait to settle into my hotel and get started.

The baggage claim area was a flurry of movement, with suitcases rolling along the conveyor belt like a parade of colorful possibilities. I spotted a bag that looked strikingly similar to mine—black with a bright blue ribbon tied to the handle. I reached for it, and just as my fingers brushed against the handle, another hand reached for the same suitcase.

Surprise coursed through me as I pulled back and looked up to see a familiar face. "Jack?" I exclaimed, blinking in disbelief.

"Mackerel?" he replied, his expression shifting from surprise to genuine joy. "What are the odds?"

We both stood there, our hands hovering over the suitcase, caught in a moment that felt frozen in time. After a second, we released our grips, laughter spilling between us.

"What are you doing here?" I asked, my heart racing as memories of our time in Alaska flooded back.

"I'm just visiting my family," he said, a warm smile lighting up his face. "I didn't know you were coming for the conference. Are you excited?"

"Yeah, I can't wait! I've been looking forward to this for ages," I replied, my nerves momentarily forgotten. "But it's so good to see you!"

"It really is," he said, and I could see the warmth in his eyes, the familiar spark that made my heart flutter. "I feel like we should catch up properly."

"I'd love that," I said, my voice a little more eager than I intended. "How about we grab a coffee before I head to the conference? There's a café nearby."

"Sounds perfect," he agreed, and we made our way out of the airport, the familiar Seattle drizzle creating a cozy atmosphere as we chatted.

At the café, we found a corner booth, the smell of freshly brewed coffee wrapping around us like a warm blanket. As we sipped our drinks, the conversation flowed naturally, filled with laughter and shared memories.

"I've missed this," I admitted, leaning forward. "Talking to you always feels so easy."

"Me too," he said, his eyes sparkling. "Alaska was such a significant time for me. I still think about it often."

We reminisced about our adventures, from kayaking to the tiny island he named Cinnamon Island to watching the fireworks on the boat. Each memory brought a smile to my face, a reminder of the connection we had shared.

"So, how's your writing going?" Jack asked, genuinely interested.

"It's been great, actually. I've been working on a story about my trip to Alaska," I said, excitement bubbling in my chest. "It feels like a piece of my heart is in that story."

"I can't wait to read it. You have a way of capturing emotions that's really special," he said, and I felt a warmth spreading through me at his words.

As the conversation continued, I realized I was reluctant to leave. The thought of parting ways loomed over me like a cloud. "I should probably get going to the conference," I said reluctantly, glancing at the time.

"Before you go, let's make sure we keep in touch. I'm going to be here for a few days, and I'd love to see you again," Jack suggested, his expression earnest.

"Yes! Let's do that," I said, my heart racing. "I'd love to catch up more while you're in town."

We exchanged numbers, and as I stepped back into the light drizzle of Seattle, a sense of excitement bubbled within me. This encounter felt like more than a chance meeting; it was a reminder of the bond we shared.

With every step toward the conference, I felt a renewed sense of purpose and anticipation. Jack was back in my life, and I couldn't shake the feeling that perhaps this was the start of another adventure—one I was ready to embrace, even if it was just in the time we had together before he returned to his family.

* * *

The conference center buzzed with excitement as writers milled about, sharing ideas, exchanging business cards, and gathering in small groups to discuss their craft. I tried to focus on the speaker at the podium, an acclaimed author discussing the nuances of character development, but my mind kept drifting. I sat in the back row, a notebook in front of me, but instead of taking notes, I found myself doodling little waves and pine trees.

Jack's face kept popping into my thoughts, his laughter echoing in my mind like a favorite song. I could still see the way his eyes lit up when we'd shared stories over coffee, the warmth in his smile as he recalled our adventures in Alaska. I shook my head, trying to clear my thoughts. I was at a writers conference, after all—I should be soaking in every word, every piece of advice.

But as the speaker went on, I could hardly concentrate. The words blurred together, forming an unrecognizable jumble. I could practically feel Jack beside me, the comfort of his presence wrapping around me like a familiar blanket. I missed him more than I expected, and the ache in my chest was unexpected.

After the session ended, I wandered out into the hallway, hoping to shake off the distraction and find my footing again. I grabbed a cup of coffee from a nearby stand, but as I took a sip, I found myself scanning the crowd, half-hoping to see Jack among the throngs of attendees. It was silly, really. He was visiting his family, not here for the conference. Yet, the thought of him lingered, a ghost of what could have been.

"Hey, Mackenzie!" a voice called out, pulling me from my reverie. It was Cassie, one of the writers I'd met earlier in the day. She approached with an excited grin. "Did you catch the last session? The one on world-building?"

"Uh, yeah. It was great," I replied, forcing a smile, but my heart wasn't in it. "What did you think?"

"Honestly, I loved it! I think I learned a lot. But you look a bit distracted," she said, her brow furrowing slightly. "Everything okay?"

I hesitated, weighing whether to share my thoughts about Jack. Instead, I shrugged. "Just thinking about my own writing, I guess."

Cassie studied me for a moment, her eyes narrowing slightly in concern. "Well, don't let it get away from you! You've worked hard to be here. How's the Alaska book coming along?"

I took a deep breath, trying to refocus. "It's coming along. I've been doing a lot of thinking about it lately, especially with everything that happened during that trip," I said, avoiding the specifics of Jack.

"Good! Keep that inspiration alive!" she encouraged, and her enthusiasm pulled me from my thoughts momentarily. "We should find some time to brainstorm ideas together!"

"Definitely! I'd love that," I said, feeling a flicker of excitement at the prospect of collaborating with her.

But as we talked, Jack's face slipped back into my mind. The warmth of his smile, the way he looked at me as if he could see right through to my soul. I found myself wondering what he was doing right at that moment. Was he exploring Seattle? Laughing with his family? Did he miss me as much as I missed him?

After we finished our coffee, Cassie and I drifted toward a workshop on dialogue. I took my seat, trying to shake the thoughts of Jack from my mind and focus on the task at hand.

But even as the instructor began discussing techniques to make dialogue sound natural and engaging, I was caught in a whirlwind of memories. I could hear Jack's voice in my head, replaying snippets of our conversations, the way he joked and teased me, making me laugh until my sides hurt. The way he listened when I talked about my writing and shared his dreams of adventure.

Suddenly, the workshop felt less relevant, and I found myself yearning for the simplicity of that coffee shop moment.

The anticipation of seeing him again, the spark of connection that had ignited during our brief encounter—it was intoxicating.

The session dragged on, and though I took notes, I felt a hollowness in my chest, an ache for something I couldn't quite define. As the instructor wrapped up, I realized I needed to reach out to Jack. To see him again, to explore this connection that was so undeniably strong.

After the workshop, I stepped outside into the cool Seattle air, pulling out my phone. My heart raced as I typed a quick message to Jack, asking if he wanted to grab dinner after the conference sessions ended for the day. The sun hung low in the sky, casting a warm glow over the city, and I couldn't shake the feeling that I was making the right decision.

No matter what happened, I wanted to explore this. To see where it could lead, even if just for one more night.

* * *

As I stepped outside the conference center, the hustle of the city wrapped around me like a familiar embrace. I took a deep breath, the salty air carrying a hint of adventure, and pulled out my phone. The day's sessions had been enlightening, but my mind kept drifting back to Jack. It felt like a life time since we'd last seen each other, and the thought of him stirred something warm and exciting within me.

I hit dial, heart racing as I listened to the ringing on the other end. After a few moments, Jack's voice came through, rich and welcoming. "Mackenzie! Hey! It's great to hear from you."

"Hey, Jack! How's it going?" I asked, trying to suppress the smile that crept across my face.

"Pretty good! Just visiting family. I actually just got back from lunch with my parents. How about you? How was the conference?" He sounded genuinely interested, and I could picture him leaning against something, a casual ease in his tone.

"It's been great! I've learned so much already, but honestly, I can't stop thinking about how much I wish you were here with me," I admitted, the words slipping out before I could hold them back.

"Yeah? I wish I could be there too. Seattle has so much to offer," he replied, his voice warm. "What are you doing tonight?"

"I'm not sure yet. Just going to grab dinner somewhere," I said, a flicker of hope sparking in my chest. "I was thinking of exploring a bit, but I don't know the city very well."

There was a brief pause on the other end, and when Jack spoke again, his tone was laced with excitement. "How about this? Let me show you around! I can take you to some of my favorite spots. We could grab a bite to eat, then maybe check out the waterfront or Pike Place Market. What do you think?"

I felt a rush of excitement at the idea. "I'd love that! It sounds perfect."

"Awesome! How about I pick you up around six?"

"Great! I'll be ready," I said, barely able to contain my enthusiasm. "I can't wait to see what you have in mind."

"Me too! I've been looking forward to this," Jack said, and I could hear the grin in his voice.

"Okay, see you soon!" I replied, hanging up with a flutter in my stomach.

The rest of the afternoon felt like it was dragging on, but I didn't mind. I was filled with a sense of anticipation as I returned to my hotel room to freshen up. I chose a simple yet comfortable outfit, a soft sweater and jeans, and let my hair fall naturally around my shoulders. I looked in the mirror and gave myself a little nod of encouragement. Tonight was going to be special.

As I waited, I found myself pacing the room, my thoughts flickering to all the moments Jack and I had shared in Alaska. The buoy swing, the picnic on Cinnamon Island, the fireworks under the night sky. Each memory was a vivid reminder of the connection we had forged, and I felt a warm flutter in my chest.

Finally, the clock struck six, and my heart raced as I heard a knock on my door. I opened it to find Jack standing there, a broad smile on his face and a hint of excitement in his eyes. He looked effortlessly handsome, dressed casually but with a certain charm that made him magnetic.

"Hey! Ready to explore?" he asked, his eyes shining.

"Absolutely! Lead the way," I said, stepping out and closing the door behind me.

As we walked together, the city lights began to twinkle, illuminating the streets in a soft glow. Jack led me through the bustling crowds, pointing out different landmarks and sharing little stories about his life in Seattle. I soaked it all in, feeling the chemistry between us grow with each step we took.

"Here we are—Pike Place Market," Jack announced as we approached the vibrant scene. The air was filled with the scent of fresh flowers and roasted coffee, and the lively atmosphere was infectious.

"Wow, it's so colorful!" I exclaimed, looking around at the stalls bursting with fresh produce and handmade crafts.

Jack grinned. "Wait until you see the fish market. It's famous for the flying fish!"

As we wandered through the market, we laughed at the quirky sights and sampled some local treats. Each moment felt electric, and I could hardly believe how easy it was to fall back into our rhythm. I cherished every second, the comfort of his presence making the city feel like home.

After we finished exploring the market, we made our way to a small seafood restaurant nearby. We settled at a cozy table by the window, and I felt a warmth in my heart as we talked over dinner, sharing stories and dreams, just like we had before.

"I'm really glad you're here," Jack said, leaning forward with sincerity. "It feels like we picked up right where we left off in Alaska."

I smiled, a flutter of happiness dancing in my chest. "It really does. I've missed this—missed you."

The night unfolded beautifully, filled with laughter and easy conversation. As we left the restaurant, the stars twinkled above us, and I felt a sense of longing for the moments we shared in the past. But tonight, there was something new—a sense of hope, a hint of possibility.

As we walked back toward the waterfront, the soft sound of waves lapping against the docks surrounded us, and I realized I didn't want this night to end. I wanted to hold on to every minute with Jack, to explore what was still between us, if only for a little while longer.

15

The conference room was buzzing with energy as I stepped up to the podium, the low hum of voices and rustling papers reminding me of just how many people were here, waiting to hear from me. I took a steadying breath, adjusted the microphone, and looked out over the rows of eager faces, trying to ground myself in the moment.

"Good afternoon, everyone," I began, my voice echoing softly in the large room. "Thank you all for being here. When I was first asked to come speak, I'll admit, I was a little nervous. Talking about the personal side of writing can feel like laying your heart on the page all over again."

A ripple of understanding laughter spread through the audience, and I relaxed a little, letting my eyes drift to the familiar, comforting faces of writers around the room. There was a kind of camaraderie here, a shared understanding of what it meant to pour yourself into your work.

"My latest project is a piece I think of as both a travelogue and a personal memoir. It's a book I wrote after spending time in Alaska—an experience that changed me in ways I hadn't anticipated. And that's what I'd like to discuss today: how the landscapes we visit, the people we meet, and the adventures we take shape us as writers, and in turn, our writing."

I paused, feeling my nerves fade as I spoke from the heart. "Alaska was breathtaking and isolating, wild and welcoming all at once. But more than the landscape, it was the connection I formed there that truly impacted me. It forced me to think about what I want, what I'm willing to risk, and how vulnerable I can be in my own work."

My thoughts flashed back to Jack and all the memories woven into that trip. I took another breath and continued, feeling like I was speaking more directly to the truth than I'd anticipated.

"When we're moved by a place or a person, when we allow those experiences to seep into our writing, we're sharing pieces of ourselves that might have stayed hidden otherwise. And while that can be terrifying, it's also where I think some of the most powerful stories come from. Because it's real. It's honest."

I glanced around the room, seeing heads nod in quiet agreement, and felt a sense of connection build. My voice grew more assured as I finished. "So if I leave you with one piece of advice today, it's this: lean into those connections, the ones that shake you up, the ones that ask you to be braver than you thought you could be. That's where the best stories hide."

Applause filled the room as I stepped back from the podium, warmth spreading through me at the response. As I scanned the crowd, my gaze landed on Jack, who had slipped into the back of the room. His expression was one of quiet pride, a small smile on his face, and in that moment, my heart swelled. Even though we were worlds apart, the memories of Alaska had somehow led us back to each other, right here in Seattle.

As I walked off the stage, a few people came up to ask questions, but all I could think about was talking to Jack, and telling him about my talk. Even at one of the most important events so far in my career I couldn't get him out of my head, and I didn't want to.

* * *

Later that evening, Jack met me in front of the Chihuly Garden and Glass exhibit. The glow of the city lights cast a warm haze over the grounds, and as I walked up, he smiled that familiar, gentle smile, the one that seemed to ease every nervous flutter in my chest.

"I thought you'd like this place," he said, gesturing toward the entrance.

"I've heard it's incredible," I replied, excitement and nerves mixing in equal measure.

He nodded, looking almost bashful as he scratched the back of his neck. "You look beautiful tonight."

I blushed and thanked him as we entered the exhibit, our footsteps echoing softly against the glass walls and the hushed murmurs of other visitors. The space inside felt ethereal, as though we'd stepped into another world made entirely of light and color.

We stopped in front of a towering sculpture, a swirl of red and orange glass spirals arching toward the ceiling like flames frozen in time. Jack looked over at me, a quiet wonder in his eyes. "I've always been drawn to this place. All the colors, the shapes... it's like someone took pieces of nature and made them into art."

I nodded, mesmerized by the way the lights reflected off each twisted piece of glass. "It's like a reminder that art isn't just something we create... it's something we find in the world around us."

We wandered through the exhibit, pausing at sculptures that looked like underwater gardens and glowing forests. In the middle of the Glasshouse—a massive space with a ceiling made entirely of glass—Jack and I stood beneath a suspended installation of glass flowers in brilliant reds, oranges, and yellows. Through the ceiling, I could see the Space Needle lit up against the night sky, framing the flowers perfectly.

"It's strange," I said, my voice barely a whisper. "I've spent so many nights staring up at the stars in New York, wishing for... I don't know, something bigger. And now, here I am, staring up at these flowers and that tower, with you standing next to me. It feels like I've found something I didn't even know I was looking for."

Jack's hand brushed against mine, and I felt his fingers close around mine, warm and grounding. "It's funny, Mack. I always thought we met because you were passing through. Like we were just meant to share one beautiful moment. But standing here with you, it feels like maybe it wasn't just a co-incidence."

My heart pounded, and I looked at him, seeing the quiet intensity in his eyes. "I've thought about you so much since Alaska, Jack. But the distance... it always felt impossible."

He let out a soft sigh, squeezing my hand. "I know. I thought so too. But seeing you here, hearing you talk about how Alaska changed you..." He paused, his voice softening. "I guess I'm just wondering if there's a way we could be in each other's lives again, even if it means taking it one day at a time."

The words hung between us, full of hope and the quiet promise of something new. I swallowed, feeling the weight of everything I wanted to say. "I don't know what the future looks like, Jack. But maybe it's worth finding out together."

He smiled, that familiar spark returning to his eyes. "Then let's start with tonight. No worries about the future—just us, here, now."

We stayed like that, hands intertwined, surrounded by the glow of vibrant glass flowers and the city lights, feeling like the rest of the world had melted away. And as we walked slowly through the exhibit, neither of us let go.

After leaving the Chihuly Gardens, Jack led me down a few blocks to a small theater tucked between a coffee shop and a record store. The faint sound of laughter and applause drifted out from inside, and I raised an eyebrow, glancing over at him.

"An improv comedy show?" I asked, a smile teasing at the corner of my mouth.

He grinned, giving a little shrug. "I thought you could use a laugh after a serious conference day. Plus, this place is pretty great. The actors are hilarious, and they're always pulling people from the audience."

"Oh no," I said, shaking my head, a mix of excitement and nerves bubbling up. "Are you planning to get us both onstage?"

He laughed, nudging my shoulder. "Maybe just you. I think you'd be great."

I rolled my eyes, but I couldn't help smiling as he held the door open for me. Inside, the atmosphere was warm and buzzing with energy. We found seats close to the stage, the theater's lights dimmed just enough to make the room feel cozy. As we settled in, Jack leaned over, his shoulder brushing against mine.

"Ever been to an improv show?" he asked, his voice low, inviting.

"Not in years," I admitted, shivering a little as his arm lingered against mine. "But I remember it being the kind of thing where anything could happen."

"Exactly," he said with a wink. "It's unpredictable—just like tonight."

Before I could respond, the show started, and the actors launched into an absurd scene about a chaotic dinner party. We both laughed as they improvised one ridiculous scenario after another, the performers reacting to each other with quick wit and over-the-top gestures. At one point, they asked for an audience suggestion, and Jack shouted, "Beekeepers in space!"

I shot him a look, giggling. "Beekeepers in space? Really?"

He shrugged, feigning innocence. "Just a classic storyline."

The actors took his suggestion and ran with it, creating a hysterical scene involving floating honey jars and bees with jet-packs. Jack and I doubled over laughing, tears in our eyes from the absurdity. And then, one of the actors caught sight of us.

"Oh, we've got a lively couple over here!" she announced, pointing us out to the audience. "How about a little on-the-spot romance improv?"

I felt my cheeks heat up, but before I could protest, she beckoned us to the stage, and Jack, grinning, grabbed my hand and pulled me up.

"Come on, Mackerel. Let's show them how it's done," he whispered, giving me a mischievous look.

We stepped up, and the actors handed us imaginary micro-phones. "Tell us," the main comedian said, "how did you two meet?"

Jack looked at me, that twinkle of mischief still bright in his eyes. "Oh, it was fate, actually," he said, launching into an elaborate story. "We met in a coffee shop in Alaska, fighting over the last cinnamon roll."

I laughed, rolling with his improvisation. "Yes, but he didn't realize that I actually hate cinnamon rolls, so I ended up giving it to him after we argued about it for ten minutes."

He put a hand to his chest, pretending to look wounded. "Hate cinnamon rolls? I can't believe I fell in love with a woman who doesn't appreciate a good pastry."

"Well," I replied, trying not to break character as I looked at him, "I guess you'll just have to win me over some other way."

The audience laughed, and Jack leaned in, his eyes warm as he held my gaze. "Challenge accepted."

As we stepped back down to our seats, still laughing, the lights dimmed again, and he reached over, his hand finding mine in the darkness. My heart raced, and I could feel the warmth of his palm against mine.

"You know," he murmured, his face close to mine, "you were pretty good up there. Maybe you've got a secret calling in improv."

"Oh, please," I whispered, shaking my head, though I couldn't keep the grin off my face. "I'd rather leave it to the professionals."

He tilted his head, looking at me with that playful expression that made my heart skip a beat. "So you're saying you don't like cinnamon rolls and don't like improv? You're really throwing me for a loop, Mack."

I chuckled, squeezing his hand. "Guess you'll just have to stick around and find out what else you don't know about me."

The rest of the show went by in a blur of laughter and playful banter, and as we walked out of the theater together, I felt a lightness in my chest, like the weight of all those years apart had lifted, even if just for tonight.

* * *

After a whirlwind week of reconnecting with Jack and diving into the conference, I finally felt ready to close the chapter I'd kept open for so long. The book I'd been writing—part memoir, part love letter to Alaska—had waited for an ending. And now, I had it.

I sat down in the quiet corner of the hotel room, my laptop still open, and picked up my phone. My fingers hovered over my editor Lila's contact. For years, she'd been the first person I'd call with updates, patiently listening as I worked through drafts, hitting highs and lows. She'd been as invested in this book as I was, and I knew she'd want to know it was finally complete.

With a deep breath, I pressed "call." Lila picked up on the second ring.

"Mackenzie!" she answered, sounding surprised and delighted. "I wasn't expecting a call from you! How's Seattle? The conference?"

"Seattle's been… incredible. It's been a lot more than I expected, honestly."

"That sounds promising! Tell me everything."

I laughed softly, tucking my knees to my chest. "There's actually only one thing I need to tell you. I finished the book, Lila."

There was a stunned silence on the other end, followed by an excited gasp. "You finished it? Mackenzie! Are you serious? I thought you'd still need more time, given how personal it is."

"I thought I would too," I admitted. "But being here, seeing people again and getting out of my usual New York headspace, I realized I had all the pieces I needed. And it's not like the story is frozen in time. I'm still living it, in some ways. But I think the book is ready to end."

Lila's voice softened. "You don't know how long I've been waiting to hear this. I know how much Alaska means to you. I remember the day you told me you were even considering writing it. So, tell me, how do you feel? Relief? Pride?"

I closed my eyes, letting her words settle. "A little of everything, I think. It feels like closure, like maybe I've finally honored that time, that part of me, and Jack, and Alaska. It's not like I'm leaving it behind, but I think I'm ready to let other people in—to share what it meant to me."

Lila sighed with warmth. "I'm so glad to hear that, Mackenzie. You know how powerful this story is. Readers are going to fall in love with it, the way you bring Alaska to life. And that vulnerability, that connection—you'll give people something to hold onto."

My heart lifted, but it was still tinged with a little uncertainty. "I hope so. I won't lie, though. It's scary. This book is all of me, and sharing it feels like putting a part of myself out there that I've never shown before."

"I get it. It's raw, and that's what makes it so beautiful," Lila replied, her voice soothing. "But if you need time, if you're not ready—"

"No," I said, feeling a surge of resolve. "I think I am ready. I needed to come back here and live a little, to see where I am now compared to where I was then. Now I know, and I'm ready to let it go."

There was a smile in her voice as she replied, "Then let's do it. Let's get this story out there. When you get back, we'll go over the final draft together and make sure it's everything you want it to be. But Mackenzie, no matter what anyone else thinks, I want you to know that you've done something amazing. You've turned your heart into words."

A rush of warmth filled me. I hadn't even realized how much I'd needed to hear that.

"Thank you, Lila," I said, my voice a little thick. "I don't think I could've done this without you pushing me all these years."

She laughed. "Well, let's just say it's been a pleasure to nudge you. Go enjoy your last day in Seattle, and maybe do something to celebrate. You've earned it."

I hung up, a mixture of excitement and nervousness thrumming through me. After all these years, my story was ready to be shared.

16

After wrapping up my last conference obligations, I felt lighter, like a huge weight had finally lifted. Jack and I had made plans to meet up that evening, and I was both excited and a little nervous when he texted to say his family would be joining us. It wasn't something we'd planned, exactly, but he mentioned his sister and a few of his cousins wanted to check out a local restaurant and invited us along.

I arrived first, standing at the entrance of the cozy waterfront spot Jack had recommended. I was scrolling through my phone when I felt a warm hand on my shoulder. I turned around, and there he was, grinning at me, looking both effortlessly familiar and still somehow new. My heart did that funny little flip it always did around him.

"Hey, you," he said, pulling me into a quick hug.

"Hey yourself," I replied, smiling up at him. "So, am I about to be put through the family wringer?"

He laughed, shaking his head. "They'll go easy on you. But if anyone asks what my most embarrassing childhood memory is, you're off the hook for answering, okay?"

"Noted," I said, grinning as he led me through the door.

The restaurant had a rustic, welcoming vibe, with big windows overlooking the water and warm wood accents everywhere. We made our way toward a large table where Jack's family was already waiting, laughing and chatting. As soon as they spotted us, they waved us over with enthusiastic smiles.

"This is Mackenzie," Jack said, introducing me to everyone. "Mackenzie, this is my sister, Jenny, and my cousins, Ava and Tyler."

They all greeted me warmly, and I felt my initial nerves begin to ease. Jenny, his sister, was immediately warm and bubbly, reaching over to give me a little hug. Ava and Tyler grinned and nodded, both with the kind of laid-back friendliness that made me feel like I'd known them longer than a few minutes.

"So, Mackenzie," Jenny said, leaning toward me conspiratorially. "What's it like putting up with my brother?"

"Oh, it's a real trial," I said, glancing at Jack with a teasing smile. "He's stubborn, has strong opinions about the best coffee beans, and insists on bringing up Alaska any chance he gets."

Everyone laughed, and Jack rolled his eyes with a grin. "Not true! I can hold off on Alaska talk if I have to."

"But do we want you to?" Ava asked, nudging him. "We've heard so many stories, but it sounds like the two of you had an unforgettable time up there."

I felt a little rush of emotion as I thought back to that summer. "It was... amazing. I mean, I think about it all the time. There's no place like Alaska."

Jenny smiled knowingly. "It's probably why my brother fell so hard for it—and, you know, maybe a certain someone he met there."

I blushed, and Jack looked like he was both amused and slightly mortified. "All right, all right," he said, chuckling. "Let's keep it civil here."

Dinner flowed naturally after that. We talked about everything from travel to food, and Jack's family told funny stories from their childhood, ones that had me laughing until my sides hurt. Jenny even pulled up an old photo of Jack in an unfortunate Halloween costume, which he tried unsuccessfully to steal from her.

When we finally ordered dessert, Jenny leaned over and asked, "So, Mackenzie, are you going to keep Jack waiting for an invite to New York?"

I glanced at Jack, whose eyes held a curious light, and shrugged. "Well, if he can handle the chaos of New York, I might be convinced to show him around."

Jack smirked. "I can take on New York," he said, his tone teasing. "As long as I have a local guide."

Jenny gave me an approving nod. "You're a keeper, Mackenzie. You fit right in with us."

Warmth spread through me as I took in her words. For a moment, I let myself imagine what it would be like if this were more than just a night out—if meeting his family and laughing over dinner was a part of my life, part of *our* life.

When we finally parted ways, Jenny hugged me, promising to make Jack bring me along to their next family gathering. As Jack and I stepped outside into the cool evening air, he took my hand, his thumb brushing lightly over mine.

"They loved you," he said, his voice soft and a little shy.

"They're great," I replied, smiling up at him. "And maybe they're right—I should probably invite you to New York sometime soon."

He laughed, pulling me close. "Just say when, Mack."

In that moment, it felt like the distance between us wasn't so insurmountable after all.

* * *

We were nearing the end of my time in Seattle, and Jack had insisted on planning one last surprise. He wouldn't give me any hints, though, despite my best attempts to pry it out of him. So when he pulled up next to the water's edge at Lake Union early that morning, I looked at him, wide-eyed.

"You're kidding," I said, laughing in disbelief. "We're going on a float plane?"

Jack grinned, his blue eyes sparkling with excitement. "I figured it would bring back a few memories. We didn't have enough time on the water last time, don't you think?"

I shook my head, half-laughing and half-stunned as I took in the small float plane waiting for us at the dock. The pilot gave us a friendly wave, and Jack pulled me toward him, clearly thrilled. The smell of salt water and the faint hum of city life around us made me nostalgic for Alaska in a way that made my chest ache.

As we boarded, I felt the same nervous excitement as the last time we flew over Alaskan glaciers. We buckled in, Jack beside me, and the pilot began the gentle taxi out onto the lake. The water rippled beneath us as we floated away from the dock, and then the plane picked up speed, bouncing slightly as it gained momentum.

Within seconds, we were airborne, lifting gracefully off the water. I felt the thrill of it rush through me as Seattle unfurled below, the city skyline stretching up like it was waving us off. The view of the city from above was breathtaking—space-age architecture beside glassy water, ferries crossing Elliott Bay, and mountains in the distance, their peaks crowned with morning mist.

Jack leaned close, his voice barely above a whisper as he took my hand. "Brings back a few memories, doesn't it?"

I nodded, glancing down at our joined hands before looking out at the horizon. "I keep expecting to see glaciers or whales, even though I know I'm just going to see highways and houses."

"Same," he said softly, smiling. "But I thought you'd appreciate it. Figured it might be the closest thing to Alaska around here."

I squeezed his hand. "It's perfect, Jack. Really."

The plane climbed higher, giving us a sweeping view of Puget Sound stretching out like a silver ribbon, islands dotting its surface like green jewels. It was beautiful, yet so different from the untamed landscapes we'd flown over in Alaska. Here, everything felt more contained, mapped out, softened by civilization.

As we flew, I felt a mix of nostalgia and something more—something that made me realize how much I missed those wild Alaskan moments with Jack. It wasn't just the setting that made Alaska special; it was him.

We flew over Lumen Field, the Space Needle, and downtown Seattle. I couldn't believe how little I felt in comparison to the sprawling city. Juneau had felt completely different in comparison. Although Seattle was absolutely beautiful, it lacked the emotional connection I had with Alaska.

After a while, Jack turned toward me, his expression unreadable. "Mack, I know it's not the same, but I thought... I thought we could make a new memory. Something to add to Alaska, but a little closer to home."

He looked almost vulnerable, like he wasn't sure if this would measure up to those memories. But in that moment, it didn't matter. Seattle, Alaska—it was the feeling of being with him, looking down at the world from above, that I wanted to hold onto.

I smiled, leaning closer to him. "Jack, this is incredible. And no matter what, we'll always have those memories—and now this one, too."

The plane began to descend, bringing us back down to the lake, and as we coasted toward the dock, I felt a quiet sense of happiness settle over me. Jack had given me a piece of Alaska right here in Seattle, and in doing so, he'd made this place feel special, too.

When we touched down, the float plane skipping lightly across the water before slowing, Jack turned to me. "So, think you'll come back to Seattle again?"

I couldn't help but laugh as we stepped back onto the dock, our hands still intertwined. "After this? I think I might have to."

After the float plane ride, the sun hung low in the Seattle sky, casting a warm golden hue across the water and illuminating the cityscape. Jack and I walked back to my hotel, the excitement from our adventure still buzzing between us. I couldn't stop smiling, my heart fluttering with every glance he shot my way.

"Want to grab a bite to eat?" he asked, his hands stuffed in his pockets as we strolled along the waterfront. The salty breeze tossed my hair around, and I felt a thrill every time our shoulders brushed.

I shook my head playfully. "After that amazing picnic, I think I'm still full! Besides, I think I'd rather just enjoy this moment."

He raised an eyebrow, a playful smirk spreading across his lips. "Oh really? Just you and me? In your hotel room? Sounds dangerous."

"Dangerous?" I laughed, feeling a rush of warmth at his teasing tone. "What are you implying, Jack?"

He stepped closer, lowering his voice, the teasing edge replaced with sincerity. "Just that I wouldn't want to keep you up too late with all my... charming stories."

I felt a shiver of anticipation as I looked up into his eyes, seeing the spark of mischief mixed with something deeper. "I think I can handle a little charm, don't you?"

With a soft chuckle, he turned us toward the hotel entrance, his presence steadying as we walked inside. The lobby was quiet, but the atmosphere felt electric, charged with the tension and excitement of what the night might hold.

Once in my room, I dropped my bag on the floor and moved to the window, pulling back the curtains to reveal the view of the city lights twinkling like stars. Jack stepped up beside me, our shoulders brushing again as we both took in the sight.

"It's beautiful," he said, his voice soft as he glanced at me. "But I think the view has some serious competition."

I turned to meet his gaze, my heart racing. "Are you always this charming, or am I just special?"

"Definitely special," he replied, his expression turning serious. "You've always been special to me, Mack."

The weight of his words hung in the air between us, a tangible connection that pulled me closer. My breath caught as I looked up at him, my pulse quickening. I felt every moment we'd shared in Alaska come rushing back—the laughter, the stolen glances, the late-night talks. Everything led to this.

"Jack..." I started, but he silenced me with a finger on my lips.

"Just let it happen," he murmured, his eyes locked on mine. "No pressure."

With that, he leaned in, and I felt the heat radiating between us. Our lips met, a soft and tentative kiss that deepened as we melted into each other, losing ourselves in the moment. The world outside faded away, and all that mattered was this connection, this feeling of being right where I was meant to be.

When we finally pulled back, breathless and smiling, I could feel the excitement of possibility in the air.

"Wow," I whispered, my cheeks flushed. "I didn't see that coming."

Jack chuckled softly, his thumb brushing against my cheek. "Neither did I, but I'm glad it did."

We settled onto the small couch in my room, our fingers intertwined, the room filled with laughter and soft conversation. As the night wore on, it felt like a dream—one that I never wanted to end. The city lights sparkled outside, and in that moment, I knew that whatever lay ahead, we would face it together.

* * *

I walked Jack out to his car, giving him a quick kiss goodbye. As soon as I got back to my hotel room, I felt the urge to call Cassie and Sarah. They'd both been there with me on the Alaska trip—listening to my endless fretting over Jack, watching me try to hide the butterflies he gave me. If anyone could help me work through this new twist, it was them.

I grabbed my phone, took a deep breath, and dialed our group call. Cassie picked up first, then Sarah joined a moment later, both of them sounding excited and curious.

"Mackenzie! Tell us everything!" Cassie said. "We want details!"

"Okay, okay," I laughed, flopping down on the bed and staring at the ceiling. "You're not going to believe this, but I ran into Jack here. At the airport of all places."

"No way!" Sarah gasped. "Is he here for work?"

"Nope, just visiting family. Total coincidence. We ended up catching up and spending a little time together, and... well, it feels like no time has passed. It's like Alaska all over again, except in Seattle."

"Wow," Cassie murmured. "So, how do you feel about it?"

"That's the thing," I said, biting my lip. "I feel... everything. I mean, it's been five years, and here I am feeling the same connection. But I'm worried about what comes next."

Sarah sighed knowingly. "You're thinking about work, aren't you?"

"Yeah," I admitted. "I'm finally getting somewhere with my career. The last few years have been nonstop writing, growing my platform, connecting with other authors... I can't imagine pulling back now. And long-distance relationships are so hard, especially with our schedules. But I don't want to just walk away from him, either."

Cassie chimed in, "It sounds like you're trying to balance two things that are super important to you, Mackenzie. Your career is your dream, but maybe Jack is, too?"

Sarah agreed. "Exactly. We all know how much you care about your writing. But you've also been talking about Jack since Alaska. Maybe there's a way to keep both in your life."

I took a deep breath, feeling their words sink in. "I know. I just don't know if I can be with him without sacrificing the momentum I've built in New York. What if one of us ends up resenting the other?"

Cassie was quiet for a moment. "You're the only one who knows your priorities, Mackenzie. But... maybe this is one of those 'trust yourself and see what happens' moments. Don't make a choice because you think you should. Make it because you want to."

Sarah added, "Think of it this way—what's scarier to you: giving this a chance and maybe finding a way, or not taking the risk at all?"

I felt a swell of emotion rise in my chest. I didn't want to look back and wonder what could have been. But the thought of balancing everything felt daunting, too. "Thank you, both of you," I said, my voice barely above a whisper. "I think... I think I'm going to take a leap of faith here."

Cassie laughed softly. "That's our Mackenzie. Whatever happens, we're here for you. Now go make it worth the risk."

"Promise to keep us updated," Sarah said, her voice filled with encouragement. "You deserve happiness, Mackenzie. And if anyone can make this work, it's you."

We talked a little longer, their encouragement sinking in and helping me feel braver. After I hung up, I sat there, the room feeling both too small and full of possibility. Maybe there was a way to have both, a life with Jack and a career I loved. For the first time, I allowed myself to believe it might be possible. Now all I needed to do was to tell everyone of my decision.

17

The following day, I scheduled a call with my editor, Lila, and my publisher. I had decided it was time to tell them that I wanted to shift to working remotely. Jack and I had been talking about it more seriously over the past few days, and the idea of starting fresh together somewhere new was exciting.

When Lila's face popped up on my screen, I was surprised by how nervous I felt. She'd been one of my biggest supporters, guiding my career since my first book, and I knew she had high hopes for my future projects. I just hoped she'd understand.

"Hi, Mackenzie!" Lila's warm smile greeted me. "What's this big update you hinted at in your email?"

"Hi, Lila. Thanks for taking the time," I said, shifting in my seat. "I've been thinking about my work-life balance lately, especially after reconnecting with someone special from my past. I'd like to move to a remote setup for a while, maybe even relocate. I think it'll give me the freedom to focus more on my writing and my personal life."

Lila's smile faded slightly, and she exchanged a glance with Martin, the head of publishing, who was also on the call.

"Mackenzie," she started, carefully choosing her words, "I understand wanting to find balance. But the way we've positioned you—book signings, local appearances, in-person events—it's all helped build your brand. Moving away could make it hard to maintain that momentum. Readers love that you're here in New York. You're part of a community they feel connected to."

Martin chimed in, his voice measured. "We've invested a lot in making sure you have these connections. Our team has plans for you, Mackenzie—a major book tour, exclusive interviews. And frankly, working remotely could make that much harder."

I could feel my chest tightening. This was the last reaction I'd expected, and I found myself clinging to their words, the weight of their disapproval sinking in.

"So... you're saying that moving could jeopardize everything we've built?" I asked, my voice sounding smaller than I intended.

Lila's expression softened. "Not necessarily, but it's a risk. I've seen authors take a step back and struggle to find their footing again. You have something special here, Mackenzie.

New York has been good to you, and you've been good for New York."

I swallowed hard, the thought of giving up the career I'd worked so hard for suddenly very real. Staying in New York would mean continuing to grow my career, and maybe even reaching new heights. But it would mean putting distance between Jack and me—risking the connection we'd just found again.

"I hadn't thought about it like that," I admitted, feeling torn. "I don't want to lose the momentum we've built."

"Take some time," Lila said gently. "Think it over. But know that we'll support you no matter what. We just don't want to see you lose what you've worked so hard to achieve."

I nodded, feeling a mix of gratitude and confusion. After we ended the call, I sat in my empty apartment, letting the silence settle. A part of me longed to follow Jack, to dive into that unknown future with him. But I couldn't ignore the reality that staying in New York was what my career needed.

And maybe, for now, it was what I needed, too. I picked up my phone, the decision weighing heavily as I prepared to tell Jack that I couldn't leave New York—at least, not yet.

* * *

Later that night, I sat on my bed, staring at Jack's contact on my phone screen. My thumb hovered over the call button as I braced myself, piecing together the words in my head. This conversation was going to hurt, and there was no way around it.

With a deep breath, I tapped the button. Jack answered after a few rings, his warm voice cutting through the silence of my room.

"Hey, Mack," he greeted, and I could hear the smile in his voice. "How'd your meeting go? Got any news for me?"

I forced a smile, even though he couldn't see it. "Hey, Jack. Yeah, I, uh... I talked to Lila and Martin today."

"Oh yeah? How'd it go?" He sounded hopeful, and it made my stomach twist.

"Jack..." I started, my voice catching. "They... well, they don't think moving away is a good idea. They're worried it'll hurt my career if I step away from everything we've built here."

There was a pause on the other end, and I could hear his breathing, steady but a little slower than before. "So... what does that mean?" he finally asked, his voice quieter.

"It means I can't leave New York—not right now, anyway." I swallowed the lump in my throat, my voice coming out barely above a whisper. "I want to be with you, Jack, but they made it really clear how much staying here matters for my future. And it's just... it's my career, you know?"

"I get it," he replied, and the sadness in his voice broke my heart. "You've worked so hard to get where you are, Mackenzie. I don't want you to give that up."

"I hate this," I murmured, wiping at my eyes. "I don't want it to be the end of us, Jack, but... I just don't see how we make it work."

He was quiet for a moment, then exhaled softly. "Maybe... maybe this is the best we can do right now." His voice wavered, and I could tell he was trying to hold it together, just like I was. "You belong in New York, Mackenzie. And I... I belong in Alaska. I wish I could be the guy who could pick up and go anywhere, but my life's here. It's everything I know."

"I understand." I tried to steady my voice. "I don't regret a second of what we had, Jack. I wouldn't change any of it."

"Me neither," he said, a mix of sorrow and warmth in his voice. "I'll never forget this, Mackenzie. Not a single moment."

We sat in silence, both of us breathing together on opposite sides of the line, neither wanting to let go. Finally, he whispered, "Goodbye, Mackenzie."

"Goodbye, Jack," I whispered back, and with a click, the call ended.

I set my phone down and sat there, the silence pressing in around me. It felt like a chapter had closed—a beautiful, bittersweet chapter that would live on in my memory, even if it couldn't be part of my future. And for the first time in a long while, I let myself cry, letting go of a love that was never meant to be, but one I would cherish forever.

* * *

The airport was buzzing with the usual pre-flight energy: families hugging goodbye, people juggling bags and coffee cups, hurried announcements over the intercom. But I felt like I was moving in slow motion as I made my way toward the gate, each step heavier than the last. My stomach twisted, and I couldn't stop glancing over my shoulder, half hoping—half dreading—I'd see Jack.

I tried to focus on all the reasons this decision was the right one. My career, my life in New York, the safety of the familiar path. But every reason felt hollow next to the ache I felt at leaving him behind.

I was almost at security when I heard his voice.

"Mack!"

I froze, my heart hammering as I turned around. There he was, striding toward me, his eyes locked onto mine, his expression a mix of determination and vulnerability. My breath caught in my throat, and for a second, I thought I was dreaming.

"Jack?" I whispered, hardly able to believe he was standing in front of me. "What are you doing here?"

He stopped just inches away, his hands sliding to my shoulders as he looked at me, his gaze searching. "I couldn't let you leave like this," he said, his voice thick with emotion. "Not without telling you how I really feel."

I swallowed, barely able to process the intensity in his eyes. "Jack..."

"No, let me say this." He took a deep breath, his fingers tightening on my shoulders. "I tried to convince myself that letting you go was the right thing—that it was for the best. But Mackenzie, I don't want to spend the rest of my life wondering what could have been. I don't want to watch you walk away again and regret every day that I didn't fight harder to keep you here. When you're not around, I feel incomplete.

I've been pretending I'm okay without you, but I can't lie anymore. Every time I look at you, I feel like I've found home... I love you more than I ever thought possible, and I'm not going to pretend otherwise anymore. I'm ready to be with you for whatever comes next. "

The words washed over me, his honesty breaking down every wall I'd built since our goodbye call. He continued, his gaze steady, voice low. "I know this won't be easy, and I know what I'm asking. But I don't care if it's messy or complicated. I want us, Mack. I want every piece of this with you."

My heart pounded in my chest, a mix of fear and exhilaration. I'd spent so long convincing myself that my career was all that mattered, that I could find happiness in my work alone. But now, standing here with Jack, I felt something shift inside me.

I took a deep breath, my mind racing. "But what about my job? My life in New York?"

Jack's face softened. "You'll figure it out. We'll figure it out together. And if it takes a little while, if it's a little rough, I'm here for it. I'm here for all of it."

A thousand practicalities flashed through my mind, but they felt small in comparison to the surge of hope in my chest. I looked into his eyes, seeing the same dreams I'd once had of finding something real, something lasting, something worth the risk.

"Screw it," I whispered, a smile tugging at my lips as I laughed, feeling suddenly weightless. "I'll move to Alaska. I don't know how we'll make it work, and I don't have a plan, but I'll figure it out."

A grin broke across his face, and before I could say another word, he pulled me into his arms, holding me so tightly I could feel his heartbeat against mine. "You have no idea how much this means to me, Mackenzie. I thought I'd lost you."

I buried my face in his shoulder, breathing him in, feeling the warmth and safety of his embrace. "You're not losing me. Not anymore."

When he pulled back, his smile was as bright as I'd ever seen it. "Let's go home, then," he said, his eyes shining with a joy that mirrored my own. "We'll figure it out, one day at a time."

Hand in hand, we walked out of the airport, leaving behind the flight, the gate, and all my old doubts. There was no turning back now. I was ready to step into the unknown with him, and I couldn't imagine any place I'd rather be.

* * *

The moment we stepped into the hotel room, a wave of nostalgia washed over me. It felt surreal to be back with Jack by my side, after all these years apart. The soft light of the lamp in the corner illuminated the room, casting a warm glow that made everything feel cozy and inviting.

Jack closed the door behind us, and for a moment, we both just stood there, absorbing the familiar yet new atmosphere. "So, what now?" he asked, his voice low and relaxed, a hint of that playful mischief dancing in his eyes.

"I guess we should start with a celebratory drink," I replied, moving toward the small fridge. I opened it to reveal a selection of bottled water and a couple of beers. I grabbed one of the beers and tossed it to him. "How about this?"

"Perfect," he said, cracking it open and taking a long swig before leaning back against the wall. "You know, it feels strange to think how much has changed since the last time we were together."

"Right?" I said, taking a sip of my drink. "It's our lives are so different now, but in some ways, it feels the same."

Jack nodded, a thoughtful expression crossing his face. "And we're different, too. Look at us, still drawn back to each other after all this time."

I felt a warmth spreading through me at his words. "I know. It's wild to think about all the paths we've taken and where we ended up. And yet, here we are."

He moved to the small table by the window, pulling out a chair. "Let's sit and talk. I want to hear everything—what you've been up to, how your writing is going, and, of course, what you're thinking about all this."

I followed him, sitting across from him as I set my beer down. "There's a lot to catch up on. I've been writing, working on this book about my time in Alaska, which has brought up a lot of memories."

"Like the memories we made together?" he asked, leaning forward, his gaze steady on mine.

"Exactly," I said, my heart racing. "It's strange how vivid those moments are. I thought I'd moved on, but every time I put pen to paper, I find myself back there, back with you."

Jack smiled softly. "I'm glad to hear that. Those were some of the best days of my life."

"What about you?" I asked, eager to turn the spotlight on him. "You mentioned you wanted to own a charter fishing boat. Are you still working toward that dream?"

"Yeah, I am," he said, his expression growing more animated. "I've been saving up, trying to find the right opportunities. It's been a slow process, but I'm determined. I want to create something special, just like we talked about."

"That's incredible, Jack," I said, feeling inspired by his passion. "You'll get there. I know you will."

"Thanks," he said, his eyes locking onto mine. "And what about you? Any big plans aside from your book?"

I hesitated, the weight of my decision hanging in the air. "Honestly? I'm still trying to figure it all out. The thought of moving to Alaska... it scares me. But it excites me, too. Being with you, living in that beautiful place, it feels right. But I also don't want to sacrifice my career."

"You don't have to choose one over the other," he said, reaching across the table to take my hand in his. "You can make it work. You're an incredible writer, and I know you'll find a way to balance it all."

His touch sent a thrill through me, grounding me in the moment. "I hope so. It just feels so daunting. What if I fail? What if I lose everything I've built?"

Jack squeezed my hand gently. "You won't. You have the talent and drive to succeed. Just take it one step at a time. And I'll be here to support you every step of the way."

We sat in silence for a moment, our eyes locked, both of us aware of the weight of his promise. I felt a surge of gratitude, knowing that whatever path lay ahead, we'd navigate it together.

"Tell me more about your dreams," I said, wanting to keep this moment going, to explore the depths of what we both wanted. "What do you envision for your life, aside from the boat?"

Jack leaned back, contemplating. "I want to share the beauty of Alaska with others, but I also want a family. I want to create a life that feels fulfilling, you know? A life where I wake up every day excited about what I'm doing. I want to be able to show my kids what I love, to teach them about the ocean, about the wilderness."

His words struck a chord deep within me. "That sounds amazing, Jack. I can totally see you as a dad. You'd be great at it."

He chuckled, a hint of embarrassment coloring his cheeks. "Thanks. I guess I've always thought about it, but I never expected to be having this conversation now, with you."

"Neither did I," I admitted, my heart pounding. "But it feels right, doesn't it? To talk about our dreams together?"

"Yeah," he said softly. "It really does."

The air between us thickened with unspoken possibilities, and I could sense the shift in our dynamic—the weight of the past mingling with the promise of the future. I felt a spark of hope igniting within me, ready to embrace whatever came next, side by side with Jack.

* * *

The next morning, the sunlight streamed through my hotel window, illuminating the room in a warm glow. I could hardly contain the excitement swirling in my chest as I prepared to make the call that would change everything. My heart raced, but I knew I had to tell my editor and publisher about my decision to move to Alaska to be with Jack.

I took a deep breath and dialed the familiar number, the phone ringing as I paced the small hotel room. After a few rings, my editor, Lila, picked up, her voice brisk and professional. "Mackenzie! How's the conference going? You've got quite a few messages waiting for you."

"It's going well, Lila. But I wanted to talk to you about something important," I said, my voice steady despite the anxiety curling in my stomach.

"Sure, what's on your mind?" She sounded curious but distracted, and I knew I had to capture her full attention.

"I've made a decision," I began, my heart pounding. "I'm moving to Alaska."

There was a pause on the other end, and I could almost hear her processing the words. "Alaska? That's quite a move. What prompted this?"

I took a moment, gathering my thoughts. "I met someone there—Jack—and we have something special. I want to be with him, and I think it's time for me to embrace this change in my life."

"Is this about your writing, too?" she asked, her tone shifting to a more serious one. "You know you have a career to consider."

"I do, and that's why I wanted to talk to you," I replied, trying to sound as confident as I felt. "I still want to write, but I'm hoping to work remotely. I know it's not the usual setup, but I believe I can make it work."

Lila sighed, the sound filled with a mix of exasperation and understanding. "Mackenzie, we've worked hard to build your brand. Moving to a different state complicates things, especially when it comes to marketing and deadlines."

"I understand that, and I don't want to jeopardize what we've built together. But I also know I can't let this opportunity slip away," I said, my voice firm. "I want to explore my relationship with Jack, and I believe I can balance my writing career while living in Alaska."

After another moment of silence, Lila spoke again, her tone softer now. "Okay, let's take a step back. We need to work out the details of your career move. I can't promise it will be easy, but if you're committed to this, we'll find a way."

Relief washed over me, but I couldn't help but feel a flicker of doubt. "You really think you can work it out?"

"I'll have to talk with the team and see how we can transition you to remote work," she replied. "But I can't promise that everything will be seamless. You'll have to be flexible."

"Thank you, Lila. I appreciate you being willing to explore this," I said, my voice filled with gratitude.

"Just keep us updated. I don't want to lose you as a client, and I don't want your career to stall. You have a bright future ahead of you, but it's going to take some planning."

"I will," I promised, a smile spreading across my face. "I won't let you down."

After we hung up, I felt a weight lift from my shoulders. While the uncertainty of my career loomed ahead, the excitement of my decision and the possibility of a future with Jack filled me with hope. I knew I had a lot to figure out, but for the first time in a long while, I felt like I was heading in the right direction—one that led to the life I truly wanted.

Jack was worth it, and as I glanced out at the bustling Seattle streets, I could see the possibilities stretching out before me like the horizon beyond the water. I was ready to embrace it all, and nothing would hold me back.

18

Two years had flown by since I made the leap to move to Alaska, and as I stood on the deck of Jack's charter fishing boat, the crisp sea breeze tousling my hair, I couldn't help but reflect on how far we had come. The sun hung low in the sky, casting a golden glow over the water, and I watched the ripples dance beneath the surface, reminding me of the way my life had transformed since that fateful decision.

Jack had realized his dream of owning his own charter fishing business, and it was thriving. The boat, a sleek vessel named The Cinnamon Dream, was filled with laughter and excitement as families and friends enjoyed days out on the water, fishing and soaking in the stunning Alaskan scenery. I marveled at the way he navigated the boat with confidence, his laughter infectious as he shared stories with his clients, and I could see the joy radiating from him.

"Hey, Mack!" he called out, his voice bright against the sound of the waves lapping at the hull. "Can you help me reel this in? I think we've got a big one!"

With a smile, I hopped over to his side, my heart swelling with affection as I joined him at the fishing rod. The thrill of the catch was palpable, and I loved being part of his world, even as I pursued my own dreams.

As I helped him reel in a massive salmon, I couldn't help but feel proud of both of us. I had published my book about our time in Alaska, and it had resonated with readers, earning accolades and a growing fanbase. My career as a writer had taken off, and I had just signed a deal for my second book—one that explored the themes of love, adventure, and the unexpected paths life could take.

After a successful catch, we celebrated on the deck, the sun setting behind the mountains, painting the sky in hues of orange and pink. We popped open a bottle of sparkling cider, toasting to our successes and the life we had built together.

"To us," Jack said, his eyes twinkling with pride as he clinked his bottle against mine. "I couldn't have done this without you by my side."

"And I couldn't have written this chapter of my life without you," I replied, feeling a rush of gratitude. "You inspire me every day."

As the evening descended, we anchored the boat in a quiet cove in Tracy Arm, surrounded by the majestic beauty of Alaska. We spread out a blanket on the deck, sharing a picnic dinner as the stars began to twinkle overhead. The sound of laughter and the crackling of our small portable grill filled the air, creating a perfect backdrop for our cozy evening.

"Do you remember the first time we came out here?" Jack asked, his voice soft and reflective.

"How could I forget? You took me to that tiny island, and I fell in love with this place—and with you," I replied, a warmth spreading through me as I recalled our adventures.

"I knew then that we were meant for something special," he said, reaching for my hand and intertwining our fingers.

And as we sat together, watching the stars shimmer above us, I couldn't shake the feeling that this was just the beginning. We had weathered storms and celebrated victories, but more importantly, we had found our way back to each other, building a life filled with love and adventure.

"Here's to more adventures, more writing, and more time together," I declared, my heart full.

Jack leaned in closer, his smile infectious. "And to many more nights like this."

I smiled, admiring the boat and the life we had worked so hard to build together. I couldn't help but think how much I liked our little life.

"I wanted to talk to you about something," he said, his eyes searching mine. "Something important."

"Okay?" I replied, sensing the weight of his words.

Jack took a deep breath, rubbing the back of his neck. His voice lowered as if he wanted this moment to be just for us. "You know how much this place means to us, right? How it symbolizes everything we've built together?"

"Yes," I said, nodding slowly, feeling a flutter of nerves in my stomach.

He pulled something from his pocket—a small, velvet box. My breath caught in my throat as he knelt down on one knee, the boat swaying gently beneath him.

"Mackerel," he began, looking up at me with a mix of love and vulnerability, "I can't imagine my life without you. You are my partner, my best friend, and the love of my life. Every adventure we've had has led us to this moment, and I want to spend the rest of my life making memories with you. Will you marry me?"

The world around us seemed to fade away as I stared down at him, the beautiful ring glinting in the fading light. Tears filled my eyes as I processed his words, my heart racing. "Yes! Yes, of course!" I exclaimed, my voice filled with emotion.

Jack grinned widely, slipping the ring onto my finger. It fit perfectly, just as if it had always belonged there. He stood up, wrapping his arms around me, pulling me close as joy surged between us.

"I can't believe this is happening," I said, laughing through my tears, feeling overwhelmed with happiness.

Jack kissed me softly, and I knew that this was just the beginning of our next great adventure together, a journey filled with love, laughter, and endless possibilities.

In that moment, surrounded by the beauty of Alaska and the warmth of Jack's love, I knew that I had found exactly where I belonged. The path ahead was ours to forge, and together, we would continue to create a life that felt like a grand adventure—a story worth telling, one page at a time.

* * *

Six years later

The sun hung high in the sky, casting a golden glow over the glistening waters of Funter Bay. Laughter echoed across the shoreline as my two kids, Mia and Ethan, raced ahead, their small feet kicking up sand as they made their way toward the buoy swing hanging from a gnarled old tree. It had become a cherished tradition for our family—one that sparked joy and nostalgia as we revisited the same places that had once brought Jack and me so much happiness.

"Come on, Mom! You have to swing with us!" Mia shouted, her eyes sparkling with excitement as she clutched Ethan's hand, pulling him along. The buoy swayed gently in the breeze, a familiar sight that filled my heart with warmth.

I glanced over at Jack, who stood a few steps behind, leaning casually against a rock with an easy smile. The sun highlighted his tousled hair and the smile that had captured my heart all those years ago. "Looks like they're ready for you to show off your swing skills!" I teased, nudging him playfully.

Jack chuckled and straightened, rolling his shoulders as if preparing for a challenge. "Just wait until they see how it's done!" He jogged over to the tree, climbing up the rocks with the agility that I had always admired.

I watched him for a moment, a wave of affection washing over me. He was still that adventurous guy I fell for back in Alaska, the one who made every day feel like an adventure. "All right, kiddos!" he called out, gripping the rope of the buoy swing. "Get ready for the best swing of your life!"

With a dramatic flourish, he launched himself off the swing, soaring through the air before plunging into the cool water below. The kids squealed with delight, their laughter harmonizing with the sound of the waves crashing against the rocks.

"Your turn!" Ethan cried, tugging at my arm. "You have to swing now!"

"Okay, okay!" I laughed, shaking my head in mock exasperation. As I approached the buoy, I felt a familiar flutter of excitement. This was a moment I had dreamed of sharing with my family—a moment where the past and present intertwined seamlessly.

"Just hold on tight!" Jack called, his voice encouraging. I grasped the rope, feeling the familiar texture beneath my hands, and pushed off, soaring through the air. The rush of wind against my face was exhilarating, and for a brief moment, I was a carefree kid again, suspended between earth and sky.

When I landed back on the ground, I was greeted by my kids, their faces alight with joy. "That was amazing, Mom!" Mia exclaimed, her cheeks flushed. "Can we do it again?"

"Of course! But first, let's head to Cinnamon Island for a picnic!" I suggested, glancing over at Jack, who was climbing back onto the shore, water dripping from his hair.

"Cinnamon Island?" he asked, raising an eyebrow. "You mean the very same place I named years ago?"

"Absolutely! We need to share it with our kids," I replied, feeling a swell of pride at the thought of our family traditions. "I'll pack some snacks. Why don't you lead the way?"

Jack grinned, a sparkle of mischief in his eyes. "Kids, who's ready for a little adventure?"

"Me!" Ethan shouted, his enthusiasm infectious. Mia bounced on her toes, her eyes bright with anticipation as we gathered our things and headed to the small kayak we had brought along.

The ride over to Cinnamon Island was a delightful mix of laughter and playful splashes as the kids scrambled for the best spot in the kayak. Jack navigated the waters with confidence, effortlessly guiding us toward the small island that had held so many memories for us.

When we arrived, I couldn't help but smile at the sight. Cinnamon Island was as beautiful as ever, with its rocky shoreline and patches of green grass peeking through the rocky sand. We found the perfect spot to set up our picnic, laying out the blanket as the kids scampered off to explore.

As we unpacked our snacks—sandwiches, fresh fruit, and cookies—Jack leaned closer, a playful glint in his eye. "You know, I still remember the first time we came here," he said, his voice low and reminiscent. "It was a pretty special day."

"Yeah," I replied, my heart swelling at the memory. "And look at us now—sharing it with our kids."

He grinned, pride shining in his eyes. "I wouldn't trade this for anything."

Mia and Ethan returned, arms full of lupine and fireweed they had picked. "Look, Mom! We made you a bouquet!" Mia beamed, presenting the colorful assortment with an enormous grin.

"Thank you, sweetheart! It's beautiful," I said, carefully taking the flowers and setting them on our picnic blanket. Jack laughed, scooping Ethan up into his arms. "What do you think, buddy? Should we make a bouquet for Mom every time we come here?"

Ethan giggled, his small arms wrapping around Jack's neck. "Yes! And we can keep going to the buoy swing forever!"

With our picnic underway, we shared stories and jokes, the island buzzing with laughter and love. As I watched my family, I felt an overwhelming sense of gratitude. Our lives had intertwined in the most beautiful way, and these moments—swinging on a buoy, exploring the island, and sharing our dreams—were the threads that held our story together.

As the sun began to dip toward the horizon, casting a warm glow over the water, I couldn't help but reflect on how far we had come. The adventures of our youth had blossomed into a family filled with love and laughter, all rooted in the beauty of Alaska that had brought us together so many years ago. And I knew that, no matter where life took us next, we would always carry a piece of that magic with us.